UNLOCKING ROSIN MANOR

UNLOCKING ROSIN MANOR

SARAH TURTLE

SAPPHIRE BOOKS

SALINAS, CALIFORNIA

Editor - Kaycee Hawn
Book Design - LJ Reynolds
Cover Design - Fineline Cover Design

Sapphire Books Publishing, LLC
P.O. Box 8142
Salinas, CA 93912
www.sapphirebooks.com

Printed in the United States of America
First Edition – May 2021

This and other Sapphire Books titles can be found at
www.sapphirebooks.com

Dedication

For Annie, always.

Acknowledgment

Unlocking Rosin Manor was originally a screenwriting project that I wanted to revisit as a novel but I was so busy that I had only completed a couple thousand words of the manuscript. Life has a way of throwing unexpected treasures at you under the disguise of tragedy. In March of 2020, I received a call to stay home from work for a couple of weeks to wait and see where things might go with this new virus that was wreaking havoc on the world. As the two weeks extended to months, and as I write these acknowledgements, into a full year, I was able to complete my novel.

Throughout the pandemic I've had the fortunate honor of being in lockdown with my fiancé, Annie. While she isn't a writer, nor an avid reader, I have affectionately dubbed her my personal human thesaurus and dictionary. Even with spell checks that constantly monitor my every keystroke, there are just some words that the advanced technology can't guess because I'm just that good at mangling words. Annie literally knew the exact spelling of every word I asked of her. I could randomly spatter out a phrase that I wanted to say just slightly differently, and she could come back with at least a few different ways to decipher what my brain was trying to translate. As much as Annie resisted the idea that she could possibly be of any quality help with the process of me preparing my story to be sent in for publishing consideration, her thoughts, opinions, and ideas meant the world to me. I think there's a hidden talent for storytelling in her soul. For this and in all things, I love her, always.

Unlocking Rosin Manor is the story of loss, primarily that of one's parents. I am tremendously fortunate to still have both of my parents in my life. For as far back as I can remember, we would take frequent trips to the local bookstore. My mother likes to reminisce about how I thought the little plastic table and chair in the children's section was my personal furniture set. Rumor has it, if my chair was previously occupied by another child, I would use my butt to not so gently knock the kid onto the floor, out of my spot. I would then settle in to read my book while the very confused and insulted kid would go off crying to their parents. I want to thank my mom and dad for turning me into a lover of books and for accepting my naughty childhood antics. I am a writer because of you.

I would like to thank Sapphire Books for choosing another one of my stories for publication. There is a sense of security and honor of being a part of an all-female run business. I almost asked Chris at the start of the editing process if there was any possibility of working with Kaycee again as my editor, but instead, I waited nervously, wondering who I would be paired with. I was delighted to once again have the best one for the job, to pick out my inability to place commas in the correct locations. In all seriousness, though, thank you, Kaycee.

Chapter One

The sound of footsteps approaching in the hallway outside of Addie's door drew her from the deep slumber that she had been settled into. She rolled onto her side and grunted with pain as a spring from the well-worn mattress dug into her ribs. She shifted her weight to a spot with more cushion to it, and let gravity pull her arm down over the edge. The knuckles of her closed hand rested on the wooden floorboards, due to the lack of a bed frame. It was a sweltering summer day, though, even in the early morning hours, so the cool from the hard surface was welcome, and lulled her back into sleep.

Rusted hinges on the door, creaking as it opened, stirred Addie once more, but only enough to flutter her eyes momentarily. The little Jack Russell Terrier dog pressed against her thigh grunted out a contented sigh and snuggled closer to her skin. The contact comforted her, and she drifted off once more.

The sound of someone taking a drag off a cigarette and a billow of smoke being blown directly into her face caused Addie to jolt upright into a coughing fit. She swatted the air in front of her face and scrunched her mouth up into a scowl. "What the hell is your problem, asshole?"

A lanky man with greasy hair down to his shoulders let his lips curl into a devilish smirk. He crouched down and leaned in closer to her. "Mason has a job for you." His eyes lowered and lingered far too long on her tank-top-covered chest.

Addie swung her arm across her breasts to cover them. She slid back a few inches, repulsed by his teeth, stained yellow, and spotted black with decay. "You can leave my room now, John."

John's lip curled up as he sneered at her. "Be down in five minutes." He stood, but on his way up, he flicked his cigarette above the mattress.

A shower of ashes rained down over Addie's body. The tiny flakes settled on her skin and the mattress surrounding her. She turned her lips to a scowl and swatted at the grey embers, directing them to the floor.

The movement woke the little dog. He sprung to his feet and a low growl emitted from his snarled mouth. Addie pressed the palm of her hand on the top of his neck and stroked the length of his body, smoothing down the fur that had raised up on his back. When he rested back down on his hindquarters and his tail wagged in muffled thumps against the mattress, she planted a gentle kiss in the space between his ears. "It's okay, Buddy."

A cardboard box in the corner of the room contained a tee shirt to cover her tank top and a pair of jeans that she had to struggle into due to the perspiration coating her skin. Propped against the side of the box was a messenger bag that she slung across her shoulder before making her way down to the kitchen. The sound of Buddy's paws thumped on the stairs as he followed close on her heels.

At one end of the kitchen table, John sat back in his chair, teetering on the rear two legs of it. An arrogant smirk was spread across his face. "Well, look who finally decided to wake up and do some work around here."

"Seriously?" Addie wanted to rush across the room and kick the chair out from under John, but she resisted the urge when she made eye contact with her boss, Mason, sitting across from him. His glare was enough of a threat to keep her in line for the time being.

"Someone's starting in with a bitchy attitude already." John made no attempt to hide the fact that he was checking out Addie's body from head to toe. "I thought we hired a woman to do this job. Why don't you start dressing like one? Show a little skin on those legs."

The same scolding glare Mason had just used on Addie promptly shut John down. Empty beer bottles and stacks of pizza boxes littered the table, but there was a space cleared off in front of Mason where he meticulously weighed out one-eighth of an ounce of cocaine at a time on a scale. He then carefully transferred the powdery substance into tiny plastic bags. Addie waited patiently until the bag he was currently filling was sealed and he motioned for her to come closer. "I have a run for you to make."

Approaching Mason while he was in the process of weighing out product required movements gentle enough not to create a breeze, which might send the fine particles flying, yet swift enough so as not to waste his time. It was a skilled balance that Addie associated with being a ninja, and she felt as though she had put in an equal amount of training for being Mason's drug runner as one might to become a martial arts master. Within seconds, she was obediently at his side, holding her messenger bag open for him to fill it.

Addie held her breath and closed her eyes for a moment. The pungent scent of the two men in a room lacking a fan or air conditioning was too much to take in, and she chose to ignore the blatant lustful stare coming from Mason. Even before she opened her eyes back up, she knew something was wrong.

The extra weight added to her own bag should have been minimal. She should not have been able to feel the difference in a couple of ounces of weight, but she found herself needing to grip onto the nylon binding of the bag to keep it from slipping out of her fingers. She peered into the bag to check the contents, while hefting it up and down slightly. It was neatly wrapped in a brown paper bag to conceal and protect the plastic one under it, but there was an amount much greater than the usual bunch of eight ball bags that she delivered. "What is this? A full kilo?"

"Half a kilo, actually." Mason took a long swig of his beer. "Thirteen thousand is the transaction price."

Addie's eyes narrowed. "Which client upped their game to dealer status?"

"It's a new customer." Mason rushed through the statement and into the next before she could object. "Deliver the goods to 86 Grant Street. The contact name for the deal is Snare."

A heat, not from passion or the temperature of the room, but from pure rage, rose from Addie's chest and burned to the top of her forehead. "Grant Street is not one of our regular drop points. Did you choose the location?"

"No, the customer wanted that spot."

The words in her mind wanted to spill out in waves as they came to her, but she wisely chose to speak slowly and clearly enough for Mason to understand the severity of the situation. "That is the first rule that you made for this," she twirled her pointer finger in the space above the scale, "operation you're running. We always pick the drop location, or else they have the advantage over us, especially considering the size of the shipment I'll be carrying."

"I don't want to lose this deal. The profit off a bulk sale is huge."

"And so is the risk." Addie gritted her teeth. "Snare isn't even a real name."

"You're always so afraid everything is a trap. That's typical for a chick, though." John chimed in his insult.

Addie refused to give him her attention, keeping her focus on Mason. "Snare literally means *trap*."

Mason rubbed his fingertips together then scratched at his sparsely grown in facial hair. "If I change the location, he might pull out of the deal."

She reached in to pull the bag back out. "Then I'm not going to deliver it."

A sweaty palm enclosed over the top of her hand, stopping her from removing the bag. "You better do what I hired you for, or you and your little mutt can go back to living on the streets."

The control that Mason held over her was undeniable, but Addie held a strong, steady glare back at his smug expression. She wouldn't give in to his demands without the illusion that she had a choice not to. "Snare, at 86 Grant Street."

Her hand was released, but it was left with a smear of moisture that made Addie choke back the urge to gag. A snicker from John's direction made her roll her eyes, even though she maintained her lack of giving him the attention he craved from her.

At the door, Buddy was faithfully by her side, wagging his tail in anticipation of following her. She raised her hand to stop him. "It's not safe for either one of us, but especially not you. I'll be back."

Outside, the sun was consuming the cloudless sky, but at least a gentle breeze made the air less stagnant than in the apartment. It was only a twenty-minute walk to Grant Street, and Addie's long strides covered the distance in well under that time. She slowed as the numbers on the buildings got close to eighty-six and approached it cautiously.

She passed an elderly woman on her way up the concrete steps and scanned the list of tenant names next to the doorbell buttons. Addie sighed, even though she knew that it couldn't be as simple as ringing a bell directly to the client's apartment. Someone with thousands to spend on drugs wouldn't be that ignorant.

Her attention then shifted back to the old woman, who was humming a pleasant tune to herself and swaying from side to side with a giant grin spread across her wrinkled face. "The name Snare doesn't sound familiar to you, does it?"

"What has this world come to, naming a child something as silly as that?"

"I agree, but it's probably a nickname."

A hand with skin so pale and thin that the blue of her veins was the most prominent feature of them waved in the direction of the side of the building. "A group of young men took my spot out back in the garden. They shooed me away like they owned the place."

"Sounds just like the people that I'm looking for. Thank you for your help."

Addie made her way through the narrow space between the two buildings, stepping gingerly on her tippy toes to avoid the broken shards of glass and other trash littering the severely destroyed walkway. She wondered how the old woman navigated this alley daily wearing the flimsy house slippers which she had noticed were currently on the lady's feet. The trash riddled path was the least of the problems on her mind, though, as she wondered just how many people were awaiting her in the *group* that the old woman mentioned.

Her question was promptly answered as she rounded the corner into a small space just large enough to squeeze a picnic table and a couple of rusted metal chairs that were firmly bolted to a slab of concrete to prevent them from being stolen. The area felt enclosed by the brick walls of the surrounding buildings, yet the sun was still able to beam down from above. The woman out front had referred to this as her garden, and Addie now guessed that her mental state must not be completely intact, although she was correct about the group of four men, who were scattered around the yard.

After a quick assessment of them, Addie determined which was the leader of the bunch. He snubbed his nose up at the others, with an air of arrogance, and yet he cowered behind them, requiring their brute force for protection. She made a direct approach for him with confident strides, yet not rushing in, at the risk of potentially causing panic. Still, the other three guys came in from all sides to form a barrier between them.

Addie didn't let the intimidating gesture stop her completely. She took a couple more steps and tilted her head so that she could get the leader's face in her sights. "Snare, right?"

He looked from one of his guys to the next. They all had confused expressions. "Have we met before?" he finally asked.

"Nope, but I have a delivery for you."

"Mason hired a girl instead of a delivery boy?"

She crossed her arms in the space below her breasts and pushed her chest out to exaggerate the size of it. "Woman, but yes, Mason sent me."

Snare eyed her suspiciously for a moment before he took a couple of steps towards the picnic table. "Place the goods here." He motioned to the table by tapping on its badly weathered surface with his knuckles.

She pulled out the brown paper package and set it in the space as close to her as possible. Snare reached for it, but Addie promptly placed her hand on top of the solid block of tightly packaged drugs. "Payment is required first."

The tip of Snare's tongue swept across his front teeth and an annoyed grunt escaped from his throat. He then used two fingers to wave one of his minions over.

An envelope of cash was flashed just under her nose and Addie turned her head away from the juvenile action. She reached up, snatched the envelope away from the punk, and validated the authenticity of the bills before he even realized that he was no longer in possession of the money. "We're good." She tossed the overstuffed envelope into her bag, but as she turned to leave, another one of Snare's men blocked her in from behind. He stood so close that the combined scent of raw onions and marijuana initiated the gag reflex at the back of her throat.

"Take a seat." Snare motioned to the guy behind her to help follow through with his demand.

Addie felt a pair of hands on her shoulders force her down onto the picnic table seat. She instinctively tensed up and resisted, but then promptly remembered how drastically outnumbered she was, and took the seat with enough conviction that made it seem as though she wanted nothing more than to stay a while.

Snare pulled a knife from a sheath attached to his belt and used the tip of the blade to slice through both the outer paper covering, and the plastic bag beneath it. He used the flat edge of the blade to scoop out a tiny portion of the coke.

Without Snare having to give the command, one of the other guys tossed a small square of plexiglass so that it landed on the table just in front of Addie. Her heart pounded rapidly in her chest when the object settled in place, but on the exterior, she maintained her composure enough to hide her startled state. He tapped out the powder onto the smooth surface and formed a thin white line with it.

"Be my guest." He swept the motion of taking a bow, using his knife wielding hand.

"Nah, I'm clean." She cautiously started to slide the plexiglass towards Snare.

He grunted his disapproval and stabbed the tip of his knife into the dry, weathered wood of the table, bringing the square to a halt. The minuscule peak of the tiny powder mountain came cascading down the sides. "This isn't an offer. Do it, or the deal is off."

The arm from the guy directly behind Addie came around her side, holding out a small metal snuff tube. She cringed at the thought of sharing something that had previously been up his nose and immediately raised her hand up to dismiss the offer. She pulled the square within reach of her face and hovered over it.

Addie had heard stories of what it felt like to do cocaine for the first time. So many of her bosses' customers had spoken of the euphoric high triggered by their first experience. It wasn't the effects of the drug on her body she feared, though, but the fact that so many addictions began while trying to chase after that elusive energy associated with the initial high. Making the daily deliveries to the same few people who spiraled down from recreational users to junkies made the reality of the dependence one to avoid altogether.

Even with the drug being readily available in her own living space, Addie had refused to give in and try it. It was simple to deny the peer pressure of a boss who'd much rather that she not become addicted to the product that she was expected to sell. If she didn't do it this time, there was no guarantee what the four men surrounding her might do. Before analyzing it to the point of talking herself out of it, she leaned in over the table, and hovered her nose just above the starting point of the line. She pressed her finger against her other nostril, sealing it shut, and snorted the length of the line.

"It's good shit, okay." She flicked the plexiglass back towards Snare. "Are we done here now?" She wiped the remnants of powder from around her nostril with the back of her wrist.

"Yeah, I'd say you and I are pretty much finished." Snare picked up the bag and tucked it under his arm, careful to keep the sliced end upright.

Addie stood, satisfied that she had completed

the deal. She cleared her throat and a chemical taste slid down the back of it, and immediately afterwards, her mouth went dry. Then the last logical and sober thought entered her mind. She needed to get the money back to Mason.

She averted her eyes down and clutched onto the underside of her bag to confirm that it was still safely in her possession. "Thank you for the deal. You know how to contact my boss for future shipments."

"Oh, I think you've misunderstood me." A maniacal laugh released from Snare. "I may be done with you, but the others aren't." He turned and sauntered his way out of the alley.

Before Addie had the opportunity to react, two of Snare's men had each one of her arms twisted behind her back. She could care less though, feelings of invincibility coursed through her veins. She felt as though she could take on all of them. She felt strong, confident, and sexy. If only she could pull her arms free. They didn't budge, though, and the third guy was now clasping his fingers around her throat. She struggled to release herself from their grasp, especially the one constricting her neck, but as strong as she felt, they just couldn't be fought off.

She gasped for air, but nothing entered, or exited. Her eyes rolled up towards the sky, taking in the bright rays that were painfully beautiful to stare directly at, and then complete darkness as she felt her body go limp.

Chapter Two

Addie's eyes fluttered open. Her surroundings weren't familiar, and nearly everything hurt. The front of her body was face down against a hard surface and her head was turned to one side. She coughed out a ragged wheeze when she attempted to swallow. She wondered where she was, and why everything ached. With the exhale of her breath, a spray of loose gravel on the ground in front of her mouth scattered up and covered her face with particles of dirt.

When the fog lifted from her brain enough to put together the fact that she was on the ground and not in a bed, the events of how she got there came rolling in slowly. She raised her head and swiped her nose across the top of her hand. The remnants of white powder smeared across her skin as it mixed with the moisture of her sweat. She repeated the motion using her other hand. There was no point in risking inhaling anymore of the substance than she already had.

Her first attempt at sitting up fully was met with agonizing pain searing up her neck. She withered back down to the ground, taking more time to better evaluate her injury. Addie lightly ran her fingertips over her throat and down her neck. It was tender to the touch and still sore to swallow. She recalled having hands clenched around her neck right before the point of passing out. "At least I won't ever be trying to chase that elusive high, since I can't remember anything good from it."

She held her breath in as she performed the most worrisome part of her check. Her hand slid down and gave a little tug to confirm that the button was clasped on her jeans. Addie then moved lower to glide up and down the length of the zipper, making sure that it was still closed. The final step was to slide her fingers down her pants and beneath her underwear. She gently explored the area by touch, thankful that nothing felt tender. Upon removing her hand and confirming that there were no signs of blood or other fluids, she offered a silent gratitude to the universe for her safety.

A little patch of yellow and green stood out amidst the bleak backdrop of gray from the concrete. Addie could feel a smile form at the corners of her mouth, as she focused on the dandelions. The hardy little flowers had grown up through the cracks in the concrete. Her moment of simple joy was deflated as she realized that this little group of weeds had to be the *garden* the old woman had spoken of.

Despite the desire to allow her body to recover, Addie knew that the beating sun and lack of hydration would take its toll on her worse than the soreness from her injuries. On this attempt, she pushed through the pain and sat up with a heavy sigh. As she managed to stay upright this time, a tightness constricted across her chest, pulling her attention away from the other pains. She brought her hand up to her sternum and let out a sigh of relief when her fingers contacted the familiar webbing texture of the nylon strap. She was equally elated that she wasn't having a heart attack as well as that her bag was still attached to her body.

Pure adrenaline fueled the rushed reaction to search the contents of her bag. With every sweep of her hand coming up empty, a nauseating feeling dropped into her stomach. She turned the bag upside down and shook it until the only item inside fell with a thud to the ground. A glimmer of reprieve flashed as Addie picked up a journal, swiped off the bits of gravel that clung to it, and set it back into the bag.

There was really no point in torturing herself any longer by checking again. The money was in someone else's possession and no matter how she would explain what had happened, it would still be her fault, and in turn, her responsibility. Addie groaned out a painful rise to her feet and headed around to the front of the building.

It wasn't much of a surprise that the old woman was still in the same spot on the porch, despite the length of time that had passed. "Hey, did you happen to see what direction the group of guys went in when they left here?" It was a long shot to ask, but Addie hoped that any information the woman could offer up would help.

"Scattered like the wind." She flicked her crooked fingers about in all directions.

It was about all Addie could expect for an answer as she saw no potential leads either up, down, or across the street from her location. "Thanks for your help," she said, stepping onto the sidewalk.

"Young people these days never take the time to stop and talk."

A pang of guilt stabbed at her. "Your garden is clear of people now."

The walk back home was physically exhausting after Addie's body was put through a beating by not only a group of men, but also by the drugs still coursing through her system. Even worse, though, was the emotional turmoil wracking her brain as to how she would break the news to her boss that he was now out thirteen thousand dollars and half a kilo of cocaine. "He's probably going to kill me," she mumbled to herself just before entering the front door.

Both Mason and John were in the living room, lounged out, watching baseball. Addie was hoping that John had migrated to another location by now, so that she could avoid the annoying commentary that was sure to accompany his presence. He, of course, was the first to turn his head in her direction. "Took your sweet time on the biggest deal of your career, didn't you?"

Mason was on his feet and inches in front of her within seconds. "Where's the cash?"

Everything she had rehearsed in her head on the walk over was forgotten. The anger she hoped would band them together as a team to keep them on her side was lost in the fear that was now breaking her spirit. "I was attacked." She could feel a heaviness in her throat, and she shook her head while attempting to hold back tears while getting out the words that could possibly spark another beating upon her. "They took the money."

The background noise coming from the television was abruptly muted. "I told you it would just be a matter of time before this bitch would fuck up big time."

"Shut your goddamn mouth." Mason's face

never broke contact with hers. "Where's the blow?" Before she could answer, his hand was using her chin to tilt her head up at a better angle to examine her nostrils. "Other than what you snorted already."

"They forced me to test the product." As the words fell out of her mouth, she felt like a whining child defending her actions.

"Tell me you still have the rest of my coke."

"They choked me and while I was unconscious, they took off with the money and the entire package." She cringed as Mason's fist tightened to the point in which his knuckles turned white. She braced her body, contracting all her muscles in anticipation of the hit she was sure she was about to take. It was better than the alternative, though, she assured herself, knowing full well that he was almost always carrying a gun on him.

"Hey, man." John's voice, annoying as it was most of the time, was a welcome break in the tension between them. "Remember that time when I didn't deliver to the right person who had prepaid?" There was a pause but without acknowledgement of his question, he just continued anyway. "You were pissed, but you gave me a week to get the money back to you."

The expression on Mason's face darted between rage and the possibility of something else. Addie sent out a silent vibe of plea for him to give her any chance of redemption at all. Just when an uncomfortable amount of silence had passed between them, a twinge of an almost evil grin flickered across his lips. "You have one week to get me the money you lost."

"Those guys are long gone because *you* went against your own rule of choosing the location. I was ambushed and now we'll never see that money."

"I don't think you get what I'm saying. I just want my money. I don't care if you spend the next week going door to door in this city looking for the dickhead, steal the money, sell yourself for it, or get a job at Mickey-fucking-D's. Just get me my money." Mason paused for a moment in his rant, then added, "I change my mind, make it *double* the amount."

The total number, twenty-six thousand, with a dollar sign in front and all the zeros at the end, flashed across Addie's mind. It was an unattainable sum for her currently. She knew it, and she was sure that Mason knew it. If she had that sort of money, or access to it, she would not be in her present situation in the first place. "Deal. I'll get you the money."

They stood for a moment, awkwardly making eye contact between the nervous blinks, until Addie had enough and attempted to pass by Mason to retreat to her room. She barely brushed by his shoulder when his arm blocked her.

"You failed in earning your keep at the house. You can come back when you get me my money."

She glared at him in disapproval but turned towards the entryway anyway. "Fine." She used the last bit of energy left in her to mask her pain as she marched to the door. Just as her hand touched the knob, she let out a shrill whistle.

On command, the pitter patter of tiny claws tapping against the linoleum floor was heard until the little dog emerged into view from behind the kitchen island. Buddy trotted over to Addie's side and sat attentively by her side. He tilted his head and stared up at her while his whole body wiggled along with the rhythm of his tag waging.

"Hold up." Mason's command boomed off the

walls of the tiny house.

Addie stopped dead in her tracks. She was steps away from her escape. A longing sensation to be free of this situation tugged at her as she looked fixedly out the little stained window on the door. It was one of the few that wasn't covered so that people couldn't see in and witness the illegal dealings happening in the house. "What?"

"The dog stays."

Her heart sank in her chest. "I'll probably need the full week to come up with that sort of cash. Buddy needs to be fed twice a day, fresh water, and taken outside every few hours. Let me take him with me so that he's not a burden on you."

Mason covered the short space between them in just a few quick paces and swept the dog up roughly in his arm. Addie reached out, desperately trying to grasp him back to her safety. During the struggle between them, there was a flash of metal and the click of a gun being cocked that brought everything to a halt.

The nasty smirk of power spread across his lips. "You have exactly one week." Buddy squirmed in his arms, but he secured him to his side. "If you don't walk in that door next Friday by noon, I will blow the little fucker's head off. After he dies and I still don't have my money, I will find you and do the same thing to you. Got it?"

Her stomach shook, fueled by a combination of rage and fear, though she spoke as clearly and concisely as she could. "You better not hurt him." She had the urge to shake her finger at Mason, but thought it was best not to have him respond rashly, especially involving the trigger.

"Oh, I won't. For one week, I'll treat him like a prince, but after that, the little ankle biter is a goner."

"You know he's all I've got."

"Exactly, and that's how I know I'll get my dough."

Addie narrowed her eyes at Mason and softened them to make eye contact with those of her faithful companion. She nodded her head with a silent promise that she'd be back for him. "I'll see you in one week."

Chapter Three

Wandering the city streets offered none of the comfort to Addie as it once did. She had used the long walks to get away, but now there was no place to get away from, and none to go back to. She had been in this exact position once before and that is how she stumbled upon the opportunity, degrading as it was, to work as a drug runner. It provided her with a roof over her head, food in her stomach, and a little extra which usually went to keeping Buddy healthy. Now, she scoured the possibilities for a way to earn in a week what took many low-income people a year to make.

The answer finally came by way of a bulletin board in the window of a bustling diner. People stood in a long line trailing out the door, just to get a seat at the local restaurant that served breakfast twenty-four hours a day. Addie excused herself past the agitated customers waiting for tables, as she made her way up the concrete steps into the retro themed business. Just beyond the greeter stand, she squeezed behind a tall café chair. The portly man seated there shook his head at the distraction from his meal, which was a portion large enough to feed four people.

The bulletin board was overflowing with layers of flyers. It was a jumbled mess depicting help wanted ads, missing pets, items for sale, bands in search of new members, and a plethora of local concerts playing in the area. The very few empty spots of the board that poked out amongst the chaos showed that large chunks of the cork below it was gouged out from years of being stabbed by push pins. Addie wasted no time bothering to remove the pin holding the ad that she had come in for and instead gave a swift tug and tore it loose.

For a long moment, she didn't budge from the spot, enamored by the quality of the ad. Instead of the typical white copier paper, it was a thicker stock of paperboard that was so soft that it felt like cotton. There was also a fabric-like texture to it that could be seen as she held it up to the light entering past the café curtains. Centered at the top was a coat of arms symbol emblazoned with a gold foil. Most notably, though, had to be the slight tint of peach color to the paper, making it truly stand out in comparison to the others surrounding it. So much consideration was put into making a simple advertisement that would have most likely suffered the fate of something else covering it, had she not removed it.

"Hey!" A shrill voice accompanied by a tap to her shoulder pulled Addie out of the concentrated trance that she had been in. A woman with a red and white striped apron used the pad of paper for taking orders to point to the line of people. "Back in line with everyone else. Crowding our space won't help you get a table any sooner."

Addie held up the ad in her hand. "I just came in for this. I'll leave now." She straightened out her shoulders and sucked in her stomach even if it wasn't necessary for her to, in order to get past the man still shoveling in his meal.

"Hate to break it to you, honey, but this information is for patrons of this restaurant only."

While she was trapped in the space between the man's chair and the wall, the pushy waitress ripped the paper she had come in for from her grasp. She inched her way out, keeping a tight grip of her bag close to her side. Too many things were being taken away from her today, and she wasn't going to risk anything else. "Please, let me just read it and I promise that I'll put it back on the board where I got it."

The waitress smacked an oversized wad of gum around in her mouth. It was clearly to cover up the smell of cigarettes on her breath, but it wasn't quite doing the job. "Are you planning on buying something here? Even a cup of coffee will do."

Addie patted down her pockets and poked around in the crevices of her bag for any change that might be trapped in there, to no avail. "I don't have enough right now, but I promise that I will come back when I can pay."

"I don't have time for this." The waitress turned on the heels of her white high-top sneakers, and Addie watched as the one good lead she had for a money-making opportunity began to disappear down the aisle of booths. Before she was able to get too far, though, a woman slid out of her seat, blocking the waitress's path.

"Oh, there you are, sweetie." The woman, who looked to be in her sixties, with hair dyed a bright shade of auburn, flagged her arm up in the air to wave someone down.

Addie looked behind herself, without seeing anyone obviously being the target of the woman's call. She turned back to see the woman pluck the advertisement from the waitress's hand with her thumb and finger, both of which had long, painted fingernails matching the shade of her hair.

While Addie was still in a state of confusion over what was happening, the woman now suddenly had an arm around Addie's waist and was ushering her towards the booth from which she had recently emerged. She was then nudged into the long seat across from a middle-aged man with a giant grin peeking out just below his bushy mustache. The woman then boxed her in by sliding into the seat next to her. She wasn't sure what to make of this weird scenario, but just being closer to the ad was reason enough to go along with it.

The waitress appeared at the end of the table, with hands on her hips and a scowl spread across her face. "Am I going to have to call the authorities to have you removed from this restaurant?" She didn't leave enough time to answer the question before she started rambling again. "We've already established that you don't have enough money to pay for a meal."

Panic hit Addie's nerves like an electric shock. She could feel her eyes widen with fear. After everything that happened already today, having a run in with the cops would be enough to push her over the edge of what was left of her sanity.

One of the woman's fingers shot out towards the waitress as she scolded her. "Now you listen here, we are paying customers and that woman is a guest of ours. So, unless you don't care about the size of your tip, I suggest you promptly bring us out another special of the day for her." She turned and flashed Addie a nod and a wink. "And warm up our coffee while you're at it."

"I'll be right back, ma'am." The sounds of the

crowded café drowned out what visually could be seen, as the waitress stomped away and slammed the palms of her hands against the swinging door to the kitchen.

"Sorry that I went ahead and ordered for you without asking, but that horrid woman just needed a little push in the right direction."

"Look, I really appreciate what you've done to help me out, but I can't afford to pay for a cup of coffee, let alone an entire meal." Addie placed her hand on the edge of the table, preparing to shimmy her way out the second the woman got her cue that she wasn't planning on being the lunch date they expected her to be.

"We overheard everything. Don't you worry about a thing dear. Just sit back," she wiggled her fingers towards the cushion of the seat, "keep this safe," she handed the ad to Addie, "and enjoy a nice hot meal on us."

Addie waved the paper between them. "You've already helped beyond measure by getting me this. I can't believe how kind you've been to a total stranger."

"I'm Martha, and this handsome fella across from us is my husband, Ed."

"It's nice to meet you. My name is Addie."

"Well, now that we all know each other, would you be willing to stay for lunch and hear a little tale of why we want to help you out?"

Martha's smile seemed genuine, and this was a public space with plenty of people around. The threat of something going as badly as it already had earlier today was minimal in a crowded room. A rumble coming from her stomach reminded Addie that she couldn't remember when she last had an entire meal that didn't consist of leftover fast-food delivery. She pressed her back against the shiny red plastic of the seat cushion and sighed as she let herself relax. "I'd love to hear your story."

Martha clasped her hands together and her eyes widened with a giddy excitement. "Let's see, I guess I'll start with Ed and I recently retiring."

"I retired," Ed added, in between bites of toast. "The only work she ever did was in slippers at home."

Martha's finger raised to put Ed in his place. "I slaved over your hot meals and clean laundry every day, so you best not tell me that I didn't do my fair share of work." When he sheepishly focused back on his food, she continued. "Anyway, we sold our house and bought an RV. We wanted to travel as much as possible before settling down for good."

"*You* want to travel. I'd have been happy staying put where we were, and relaxing."

Martha rolled her eyes. "So, we came to this area a few days ago for some sightseeing, but our RV broke down while driving through. The repairs would have cost us a large chunk of our savings and left us without much traveling funds."

Ed pushed a fry into his mouth and licked the grease from his fingers. "*My* savings. You spent all of the money I gave you on those little animal statues that were displayed all over the house."

"Those are collectibles, Ed."

"The only thing they collect is dust, and now I'm paying rent to keep them in storage."

"I'm about ready to put you in storage if you keep interrupting my story." Martha's sharp threat sent Ed back to his meal. "So, anyway, we were lucky enough to come across a young man still in mechanic school. He was willing to fix it for his class credit just for the cost of the parts."

"That was generous of him." Addie reflected on how she had lately been spending too much of her time around people who only cared about what was best for themselves.

"Yes, he saved us a bundle." Martha placed her hand over her heart. "When we overheard how unnecessarily rude that waitress was being towards you, we thought it would be the perfect opportunity to pay back the kindness shown to us."

"How could I possibly turn down a free meal after a great story like that?"

Martha clapped her hands together rapidly. "Oh goodie!" She then pressed a finger to the advertisement. "Is this your next stop?"

Addie slid the paper in the center of the table so that all three of them could see the ad that read: *Position available at Rosin Manor. Odd jobs required for upkeep of general property maintenance. Payment includes free room and board. Apply in person.*

"Martha and I are picking up our RV later today and driving in that direction tomorrow. It's a good couple of hours away from here. Would you like a ride?"

"Seriously?" Addie looked back and forth between the couple. "Are you sure that I wouldn't be inconveniencing you in any way?"

"Of course not, dear, and besides, I picked up a flier for a lovely antique shop just beyond where you are headed." Martha raised her finger to silence her husband from another snarky comment. "We have a guest bed in the RV if you need a place to spend the night."

"I'd love to join you, then." Addie lounged even farther back into her seat. She inhaled the scents of all the different foods surrounding her, and patiently waited for her meal to arrive.

Chapter Four

Just one day after meeting Ed and Martha, Addie found herself saddened to be waving goodbye to them from the door of their RV. In the short period of time that she got to know them, she found a great respect for the couples' goal of spreading the kindness they had received from others in return. She hoped that someday, she might be in the position to be able to do the same for someone else.

An immense iron gate, not only in height, but extending out in either direction for as far as Addie could see, guarded the manor at the roadside. As the RV pulled away, the property across the road from the manor revealed to be nothing but a dense forest of trees. It was such a stark contrast from the city and suburban backdrops of buildings that surrounded her recently. She closed her eyes and allowed her lungs to fill with the fresh air given off by all the greenery.

A gentle breeze rustled the leaves and tickled her with a cool sensation that raised little bumps all over the skin of her bare arms. A chirping bird whistling out a tune brought her back to the present moment. "I can't let myself get too used to this. One week and I need to be gone," she regretfully reminded herself.

Addie approached the gate and searched the keypad. She pressed the doorbell button and waited. The whirring sound of a tiny motor just above her caught her attention. She arched her head up to catch a tiny camera scanning the area in front of the keypad. When it homed in on her location and paused, she awkwardly flashed it a wave followed by the peace sign.

A male voice chimed in over the speaker of the intercom. "Rosin Manor; how may I help you?"

She searched the pad again to see if there was something to press in order to respond, but nothing obvious popped out to her. She leaned in so that her lips were hovering just above the grooved line of the speaker. "I'm here about the job opening that was posted in the ad."

"Ah, yes. Please follow the driveway down to the left side of the manor and someone will meet you to valet park your vehicle for you."

Addie scratched at the back of her neck as she fought off the embarrassment building in her. "I don't have a car."

The motor started again as the camera searched the area surrounding where she was standing. It moved back to her once more and the voice returned. "Then I'll send a driver to pick you up."

It took a moment for Addie to fully comprehend what was just offered to her. "It's no problem. I can just walk." She waited for a response but there was nothing coming through. She tapped the intercom speaker. "Hello? Anybody there?" A loud clanking of metal hitting metal snapped her to attention as the gates separated to open the entrance to the driveway. She shrugged her shoulders in assumption that she was heard and started on her way towards the manor.

Even squinting to get a better look, it was difficult to see the manor from the end of the driveway. Not only was the distance an issue, but many large

Japanese maple trees with bright red leaves obstructed her view. A few steps in, she noticed how perfectly manicured the lawn was, right up to the edge of the tar she was standing on. She knelt and ran the palm of her hand across the top of the grass, then plucked a single blade up. After concluding that it was indeed real grass, she marveled at how it was so perfect that a round of golf could be played on it.

She had just gotten back up on her feet when a long stretch limousine came to a stop right in front of her. She rolled her eyes and shook her head at how ridiculous this was. She made eye contact with the driver as he slid the window down. "The walk isn't too far. I don't need a ride."

The driver's door opened, and a man dressed in a full chauffeur suit, including the hat and white gloves, stepped out. He made his way to the door at the rear of the car and opened it. "Ms. Rosin insisted that you be escorted back."

Addie fought the absurdity of the situation and slipped into the back of the car, avoiding the driver's extended hand to help her in should she need it. The door shut behind her and she sat in one of the leather seats, which was long enough for her to lie down and stretch out on if she had wanted to. The other seats that ran the length of the limo were spacious enough for multiple people to join her.

A tinted panel separating the front of the vehicle from the rear, descended. "There is freshly squeezed lemonade or sparkling water available in the refrigerator in the center console, if you would care for some."

"Overkill for a thirty second ride, but thanks."

Addie had expected the driver to pull out of the driveway and turn around in the road, but instead the gate closed shut in front of them. The limo jerked slightly as it shifted into reverse. She watched out the window in amusement as they crawled slowly backwards the entire length of the long driveway. As silly as this process was, she was still impressed by the skills of the driver to maneuver such a vehicle without wavering from the narrow path of pavement.

As they neared the manor, the car curved back onto the circular turnaround of the driveway. When they continued, now moving forwards, the limo bounced about as the road transitioned into cobblestone. In the center of the circle was a giant water fountain statue of Poseidon surrounded by a cluster of Sirens. The car came to a halt just in front of the entryway. Addie scooped up her bag and slid to the door, but she wasn't surprised that the driver had beat her to opening it. This time, though, he seemed to take the queue that she didn't require his assistance, as he stood back to wait for her to step out on her own accord.

The driver swept his hand in the direction of the door. "Please enjoy your visit to Rosin Manor." He tipped his hat and got back in the car. He then took off towards a row of garages which ran alongside the main structure of the building.

The manor itself stood just two stories high, but it was wide enough to make seeing the entire structure impossible from as close as Addie was standing to it. She admired the large gray stones that formed the exterior walls. It gave the manor the quaint atmosphere of a cottage, while simultaneously exuding the regal look of a castle. On her way up the few steps that led to the tall wooden doors, she ran her fingers along one of the columns supporting the balcony just above her.

At the entrance, there was no sign of a bell to ring, only a thick metal door knocker in the shape of the three-headed hound, Cerberus. She reached up to use it, but the door opened before she even touched it.

An elderly man in a suit gave her a warm smile and stepped aside. "Welcome to Rosin Manor. Please enter."

She scooted past him, cautious to make sure that her sneakers were not leaving any sort of mess on the freshly polished tiles. It was embarrassing enough that she was lacking the proper attire for a job interview. There was no way that she was going to ruin such a pristine floor. She reached into her pocket and pulled out the advertisement and unfolded it. "I'm here about the job."

"Yes, please, step into the office." He nodded towards the first of many doors down the long hallway.

Addie made her way to the office, marveling at the openness of the main entryway and the enormous staircase that led to the second level as she passed. The man who greeted her had not only carefully closed the front heavy door, as well as the one to the office, but was somehow now pulling out the chair for her to sit. For a split second, she had considered cracking a joke about how the staff here were all overly diligent at their jobs, but she promptly dismissed the idea, thinking that it might hinder her chances of getting hired. When she looked back to see where he was, though, she found that he had already left the room.

The tall leather chair, with its back to her, turned slowly to reveal a different man, not surprisingly also wearing a suit. He clasped his hands together and critically gave her the once over. "Welcome to Rosin Manor. I am the manager, Gregory, and you are, Ms.?"

"Oh, uh, I'm Addie."

"I see, well, Addie, do you have a copy of your resume with you?"

"I don't."

"No problem, then." He opened a drawer on the other side of his desk and pulled out a sheet of paper. "Just fill out this application."

She searched the space on the desk in front of her for a pen, but there wasn't one in sight. She heard an annoyed sigh come out of Gregory before he slid something over to her. Addie knew that she was very unprepared for this situation, but she didn't think that it was really all that inappropriate to borrow a pen in an office. When she reached for it, though, she realized that he had offered her a quill pen and bottle of ink. She glanced up at him to see the smirk that he wasn't doing a good job of hiding, she assumed because he probably wasn't trying at all.

She ignored the delight that he seemed to be getting out of thinking that she might struggle with the tools she was offered. Instead, she grasped the quill, dipped the tip of the nib in the bottle of ink, and began to write. After a couple of minutes, she slid the application back over to Gregory.

He glared at her suspiciously, which was understandable, due to how quickly she had completed the form. He pushed his glasses farther up the bridge of his nose and glared at the sheet. His fingertips turned white from squeezing the paper between them. Gregory placed the application back on the table. "There is next to nothing filled out here."

"Most of my adult life has been spent in college."

"Hmm, yes, supposedly you attended Harvard University in a pre-med program, but you checked off that you don't have a degree."

"I unexpectedly lost funding and had to drop out before graduation."

"Okay, well according to the date listed, that was years ago. What have you been doing in the meantime?"

"Working. It's listed there." Addie reached over and tapped the Work History column.

"Oh, I've read it already. It states delivery person, but it doesn't say where, and the little box which asks if we may contact your employer is checked *no*."

"The job posting was for odd jobs and general property maintenance. I'm sure that I could manage to figure out how to do what you need done without experience."

Gregory folded his hands on the desk in front of himself. "I don't doubt that you may be able to do the tasks required of you, but I just don't believe that this is quite what you are looking for in a job."

"I'm pretty much desperate for anything at the moment."

He once again gave her a condescending glance at her casual clothing choice. "*That* is obvious, but if money is what you are looking for, Rosin Manor is not the place for you."

"I wasn't expecting six figures or anything. Really any income at all will help."

"That is precisely where I was headed to next. You see, employees here only get room and board, free medical, and essentially any sort of material item you desire, within reason." He sat back with a smug look of satisfaction.

Addie hated the idea that Gregory thought he was successful at deterring her from a position there.

It wasn't as though she could do anything at all to earn enough money in one week to pay back her debt, but she did need a place to crash while she figured it all out. "Sounds great to me."

His eye twitched and he pursed his lips together. "I forgot to add that you would not be allowed to leave the grounds of Rosin Manor at all during time of employment. Doing so would immediately end your time here."

Those were interesting terms for a job. She questioned both the legality and the reasoning behind rules of essentially becoming a prisoner of the property. Addie kept the thoughts in her own mind, though, to avoid giving him the impression that she wasn't on board with the rules. She sat back in her chair and gazed out the window to the sprawling beautiful yard. It seemed more like a vacation than how she had been living lately. They didn't need to know that she only planned on being there for a single week before returning to her old life. "Sounds like a lovely opportunity."

Gregory released a long, slow breath through his tightly clenched teeth. "Look, Ms.," he referenced the paper once more, "Addie, with *no* last name, for the safety of the lady of the house, I cannot hire someone lacking valid credentials."

It came as no surprise that she wasn't going to be offered the job, but it still stung to get rejected. "It's evident you've made up your mind about me. Before I leave, may I ask how long it's been since you left the manor?"

"Seven years."

She rose out of her seat. "Then I guess it's not necessary for me to apologize for wasting your time."

She flashed him a wink on her way to the office door.

Addie could hear a frustrated groan behind her, followed by a quick two claps of his hands. She almost turned back to respond to the odd signal, until the door opened and realized that the man who had let her in before had been summoned to see her out.

The elderly man looked at her with a soft smile and a tilt to his head that showed compassion for her situation. "I'll have the driver meet you out front, Miss."

"Thank you, but I can walk." She headed toward the entrance.

"Are you sure? You could have a cold beverage on this scorching day."

"That is exceedingly kind, but I have a much longer walk ahead of me once I reach the gate. I may as well not get used to the luxury from the start."

"Very well then, Miss." He pulled the handle to the front door and held it open for her. "I hope your journey is a good one."

Chapter Five

Addie hung her head as she stood on the front steps of the Rosin Manor entryway, not wanting to look out at the picture-perfect view. She hadn't considered the idea that the job might not pan out the way she hoped it would. Not only was she far from the city, but even if she could get back to it, there was no place for her to go.

She remembered the forest across the road and thought back to what she had learned in summer camp as a child. Possibly her skills could help her survive through the night, but there definitely wasn't enough time left in the day to build a shelter to keep out the mosquitos, which were sure to make a feast of her body. The best chance she had was to hitchhike back to the city and search out one of the women's-only homeless shelters.

Just as she made the move to step out from under the overhang of the balcony, she could hear a woman's voice coming from an open window above her. "Who was here just now?"

Gregory's voice answered her. "A woman was here about the job posting from those silly fliers you had mailed out. I told you, we should advertise on professional websites, not in shady, low-class establishments."

The insult stabbed at Addie's ego. She was grateful she didn't have to work at the same place, or even worse, *for* this rude man who thought he was better than her because of his suit. She raised her head and started up the driveway.

Only a couple of steps out, though, the woman's voice echoed even louder from the window. "I've tried that in the past. To commit to working here, someone would have to want to leave their life behind. I'm not going to find a person searching out a lucrative career. Let me guess, she laughed at you when you told her that she wouldn't receive a paycheck."

Gregory's voice was slow to answer. "No, she seemed fine with it."

"Surely she left the second you informed her that she could never leave the manor while she worked here?"

He cleared his throat. "Oddly enough, she was okay with that too."

"Then why is she leaving?"

Addie paused and turned to scan the upper level of the manor windows. She squinted her eyes against the sun's glare. The silhouettes of two figures appeared in her sights at an open window, but neither one was faced in her direction. They were locked in conversation with one another.

The shadow of Gregory's hand extended out in plea. "There is no one to contact to validate her application. She didn't even provide a full name, and she clearly did not attend an Ivy League school, like she claims. She is clearly homeless and would be unpredictable behind these walls."

His description of her just destroyed any glimmer of hope of a second chance, regardless of whether it was true. She turned once again and increased her pace double fold to avoid overhearing any more insults about herself.

Addie continued up to the gate at a speed that suggested she was on a mission to get out as soon as possible, but not so fast that it exuded that she had done anything questionable on her way out. Gregory had already profiled her as an unsafe person. She didn't want to start acting as though she had already done something that she hadn't.

When she reached the closed gate, she realized she was just as locked in as anyone would be on the outside. There was a keypad to exit that was identical to the one she used on the opposite side. She waved at the camera, hoping that someone would just automatically open it to let her out, until she remembered that it had been Gregory's voice who had opened it the first time around. She figured that he must still be discussing how horrible the interview had gone with the woman he was speaking to. Frustrated over the whole situation, she pressed the intercom button with a firm jab.

After waiting for what seemed like an eternity, and still hearing nothing but silence on the other end, she started pressing anything that looked like it would send an alert to the manor that she wanted out. "Hello? If anyone can hear me, can you unlock the gate before I climb my way out?"

"Pardon me."

Addie just about leapt out of her own skin as she noticed the figure standing behind her. She recognized him as the driver from earlier, and upon turning completely around, she also saw that in her distracted state, he had driven the limo up the driveway. She placed one hand over the location of her heart to help calm her nerves and compose herself. "You scared the crap out of me.”

“Sorry to startle you, Ms. Addie.”

“It’s okay.” She waved her hand in front of her face. “Did they send you to open the gate for me?”

“There was a request to escort you back to the manor.”

“What for?”

“You are being offered a position here.”

Addie shook her head. “I’ve already determined that Gregory has insulted me enough that I don’t want to work for him.”

The driver’s eyes got lost in the crow’s feet that grew with his smile. “If it helps, it was Miss Rosin herself who asked me to bring you back.”

Addie could feel her mind shift from defensive to confident. The thought of Miss Rosin herself deciding, even though she had heard the worst about her from Gregory, made the idea of staying worthwhile. If anything, she would have the satisfaction of watching him squirm when she walked back in. “In that case, maybe I will return with you.”

※ ※ ※ ※

After nearly an hour of filling out paperwork, with Gregory practically pulling out his hair over how little she was providing him, Addie walked out of the office, secure that she at least had a roof over her head and free food for the time being.

The kind elderly man, who Gregory referred to as the butler, met her at the door. “I’ve been given the honor of showing you to your room, but due to the lack of applicants for the job, we didn’t prepare one ahead of time. Where can we send a moving company to in order to pick up your belongings?"

She tugged at the strap of her bag. "Pretty much everything I own is with me."

"Not to worry. That is the wonderful thing about living here." He raised his arms up towards the high ceiling in the hallway. "Everything you could possibly need is under this roof." He added a wink. "And anything you'd like to have is earned with some elbow grease by doing your job to keep this place in order. What exactly is your position, by the way?"

"A mixture of whatever I'm needed for, I guess. The flier mentioned odd jobs, but nothing was described in detail, and Gregory was just as vague about it."

"Well then, how about I take your bag to your room, and send you in to meet some of the others while they are prepping for dinner?"

Addie gripped the handle to her only possession and pressed it tightly to her body. "I hardly notice it's there."

"If you'd prefer to keep it on you for the time being, you may, but please know that I would keep it safe and sound." He winked and nodded his head in the direction of Gregory's office. "Prying eyes would not lay a hand on it. I promise."

She allowed her shoulders to drop and took in a deep breath. With the exhale, she slid the strap down and handed it over to him. "No better time than now to learn to trust."

"I'm honored to earn that trust from you." He bowed his head and smiled. "Now, the door at the end of this hall to the left is where you should head next." Within seconds, he disappeared up the flight of stairs that she was so eager to explore at some point.

The hallway that she was currently strolling down was equally impressive, though, with its museum quality oil paintings lining the walls and even some bronze sculptures on pedestals in between them. The common theme on all the artwork appeared to be Greek mythology. The collection was a spectacular one for a private owner to have so many originals.

At the last door on the left, she gave it a couple of tugs, and then a push, before she realized that it was just too heavy and required a bit more of her body weight in order to get it to open. While the ancient doors in the manor were aesthetically pleasing, they didn't offer the convenience of the modern ones. Having no idea what she was walking into, she cringed as a room full of people were faced in her direction, all of which most likely watched her earlier failures of attempting to open the door. Had they all just continued to stare, she might possibly make the decision to turn and leave, but one voice cut through the awkward silence.

"Hello there." A woman with short, curly, brown hair, intertwined with strands of gray, greeted her with a wave, from behind a long kitchen island. "You must be the newest member of our household."

She strode over to the counter and extended her hand. "I'm Addie. Nice to meet you."

The woman set down her knife to exchange the shake, but then held up her soiled hands. "Berry juice all over me. I wouldn't want to stain you." She went back to cutting. "My name is Lisa. I'm the cook for Rosin Manor. Have you had dinner yet?"

She pressed her hand to her stomach. Going from years of scraping by on what she could get, to suddenly having not one, but two full meals in a single day, felt overwhelming compared to the empty feeling that used to be there. "I'm not really hungry."

"The staff will be gathering at that table for dinner just as soon as I finish the last few touches of Miss Rosin's meal." Lisa used the tip of her knife to point to a round table in the corner of the room. "You are welcome to join us, even if it's just to meet the others."

"Do you need any help with this?" Addie waved her fingers over the cutting board, hoping that her offer wouldn't involve actual cooking, of which she had little to no skills in.

Lisa didn't answer immediately as she took the time to concentrate on balancing berries on the lip of a glass of freshly squeezed juice. "Perfect," she announced, clasping her hands together, upon completing it. "Since our butler, Henry, is preparing a room for you to sleep tonight, would you mind delivering this tray to Miss Rosin?"

The thought of delivering something legal and safe was comforting. "Of course."

"Thank you dear. Just bring it through the door straight across the hall."

"Sure thing." Addie gripped the handles of the silver tray and lifted it from the countertop. The weight of it was unexpected until she recognized that it must be made of real silver. She steadied the tray so that the berries wouldn't fall off the edges of the glass and made her way to the door. This time around she made sure to use more power to open it.

"Oh, and don't forget to bring back the lid after you lift it for her." Lisa made the motion of pulling off the shiny silver dome covering the plate of food.

Addie took a deep breath before opening the

door to the dining room. She didn't know what to expect of her new boss, other than a gratitude for giving her a chance that was literally life changing for her at such a low point in her life. The way the other people at the manor rushed around like busy worker bees made her wonder just how demanding this woman might be. Although, compared to working for Mason, anything had to be better.

Stepping into the dining room was like entering the medieval times. Each of the corners of the room had full displays of armored knights. The walls were decorated with swords and maces. The most impressive piece of furniture, though, was the gorgeous solid oak table that seemed to fill the entire room. To match it were the high-backed carved chairs that looked like thrones fit for a royal family. They were so large, in fact, that she almost missed the small figure seated in one on the side at the far end.

For a moment, Addie was frozen in place at the stunning woman with black hair falling to just above her shoulders and gazing at her with deep brown eyes. She was brought out of her trance when the woman beckoned her over with a wave of her hand.

Addie hastened her pace over to the table while still focusing on balancing the berries. As she lowered the tray to set it down, it began to shake. It was difficult to tell whether it was from her forearm muscles being overexerted by the weight, nerves, or a mixture of both, but either way it was still embarrassing. "Lisa asked me to bring this to you."

"So, Addie, they have you working already."

She shrugged her shoulders. "I offered. No better time than the present to start earning my keep. I wanted to thank you, by the way, Miss Rosin, for allowing me this opportunity."

"Please, it's Nora." She extended her hand out.

Nora's hand was soft and warm. Her skin was like velvet and it made Addie self-conscious of her own, which hadn't seen a bottle of lotion in way too long. She had half expected Nora to be shallower with her handshake, as if there would be little to no importance in making a first impression on an insignificant attendant. Instead, there was firmness to her grip, which was strong enough to confirm that there was a validity in her position. Nora's other hand closed over the back of hers to represent a gentler side that showed an understanding that she cared.

The gesture caught Addie off guard momentarily. She interrupted the long pause by clearing her throat. "I apologize; everyone I have met so far has been very formal with your name."

"Most of them have been working here for longer than I've been alive. It's difficult to change something so ingrained in their minds. Once you get to know each of them better, you'll see how they love their habits and routines, making change nearly impossible." She popped one of the plump blackberries from the lip of the glass into her mouth and closed her eyes as she seemed to cherish the fruit. "Speaking of which, they are probably waiting for you to join them for dinner."

Addie glanced down the length of the long, empty table. "Isn't eating by yourself lonely?"

The shift from contentment to the recoiled reaction of having an insult slapping her flashed across Nora's face. "Maybe, just as my staff, I, too, like things as they have always been. Family and guests eat in here, and everyone else is free to dine wherever they please."

"I apologize. I had no right to ask you that. I'll leave you to your meal now." Addie rushed to leave, but just as she had almost cleared the room, she remembered what Lisa had instructed her to do. With clenched fists, she sucked up her want to jump out of her own skin and approached the table again. "I'm sorry, but Lisa asked me to bring the lid back in the kitchen." She looked down to get permission to reach across to remove the lid, but as she did, she caught sight of a stream of tears running down Nora's cheek.

Nora pulled up the napkin from her lap and averted her face in the opposite direction, while she swiped the tears away. "Just take the whole thing back to the kitchen. I'm no longer hungry." The immense weight of the chair could be heard as she slid it back to stand up and leave.

Addie's chest felt heavy. "Look, I messed up, but please don't go."

"It's fine. Just take it away, please."

She desperately searched her mind for the right words that would fix the repercussions of her ignorant remark, but before she could come up with anything short of just straight out begging, Nora was long gone.

"Damn it!" Addie flicked the side of the silver dome lid with her finger, flinching from the sting of it immediately afterwards. "Oh, but Miss Rosin, it's a shame that you didn't even get to taste your delightful meal of," she raised the cover up and felt her eyebrows mirror the motion, "chocolate cake and ice cream."

She crept her way back into the kitchen, opened the door just wide enough for her to slip through, and slid the tray on the counter, obscuring it from view behind a pile of other dirty dishes. When the coast was clear from potentially being questioned about the food being returned, she strolled over to the table that was bustling with conversations amongst those sitting around it. A hush came over them as soon as she neared.

Lisa tapped the empty seat next to her. "Come and have a bite to eat." She addressed the group sitting around the table. "For those she hasn't met yet, I'd like to introduce the newest member of Rosin Manor, Addie."

A man with a long, unmanicured beard, wearing grubby overalls, set down the bowl that he had been slurping from. "You mean our new cell mate."

"Don't be so harsh, Roger. I've never known you to step foot off this property even when you could." Lisa scooped a heaping ladle full of steaming stew into a bowl and set it down on the place setting where Addie would be sitting.

"Oh, no thank you." She refused the bowl as she slunk down into the seat.

"Silly me, I forgot to ask about your dietary restrictions or allergies. Are you a vegetarian?" Lisa aimed the soup ladle across the table towards a woman with long blond hair. "Ruth isn't a meat eater either, but I can whip you up a salad and black bean veggie burger like I did for her this evening." She moved as though she was about to get started with the process at that very moment.

"The stew smells amazing. It's just been an overwhelming day and I'd like to pass on a big meal."

Lisa's eyes got wide and she snapped her fingers. "I could heat up some beef broth. That would be less heavy on the stomach."

Addie pulled a warm roll from a basket in the center of the table. "This will do."

Henry, who was on the other side of her, gave her a little nudge with his elbow. "Our chef doesn't know what to do with herself if she isn't feeding someone."

She took a bite of the roll. "Mm. This is the best bread that I've ever tasted."

Lisa flailed her arms up with excitement, then slid a wooden bowl closer to Addie. "Spread on some of my freshly churned butter. It's sweetened with honey and a few shakes of cinnamon for flavor."

Just to appease her, Addie smeared a pat of butter on her bread. Sitting around making small talk with her new co-workers was the last thing she wanted to be doing, though, as she kept replaying the conversation with Nora repeatedly in her mind. If she knew where her room was located, she would have excused herself to it for the duration of dinner, at least.

While she felt as though all eyes were on her, she allowed her eyes to wander to the huge windows that provided a view of the manor's backyard. She slouched farther into her chair, letting the vibrant green of the lawn put her into a meditative state. She vaguely heard someone ask her a question, but movement out the window caught her full attention. A figure with a swish of shiny black hair, which the breeze was dragging up in the air, was headed away from the manor.

Addie stood, placed a couple of rolls onto a cloth napkin and pulled the corners up to wrap around them. "It's a beautiful evening for a picnic, don't you think?" She didn't wait for a response, not wanting anyone to get the idea that she intended her announcement to be an invitation, and quickly made her exit.

Chapter Six

The interior of Rosin Manor proved to be like a series of mazes that continually led Addie to the same dead ends during her search for an exit to the backyard. After multiple attempts, she chose just to return to the front entrance and follow the perimeter of the building. Having never owned a vehicle, she was accustomed to getting around by foot, but by the time she had traversed the long borders, she needed to pause to catch her breath and rub at the burning sensation in her thighs.

Addie approached behind the white wooden bench that Nora was sitting on. When she neared, she could see Nora's arms were folded across her chest. She hesitated at the body language, which suggested that no one, especially her, was invited near. She retreated backwards one step, hoping to avoid being caught in her peripheral view.

"If you're lost, there are plenty of other people who can give you a tour of the place or point you in the right direction."

Addie cringed at her lack of stealth. "I do admit, it's difficult to find an exit out of that place."

"Well, that's a new record, but I can understand there must be a million reasons why you'd want to leave so soon."

"I meant an exit to get out *here*." She pointed to the bench. "I saw you through the window and

I thought that I might bring you a peace offering." Addie held out the bundle of rolls and let the napkin fall open so that Nora could see. "May I join you?"

There was an awkwardly long pause, then Nora slid over to the far side of the bench, although there would have been plenty of space had she not moved aside. "Lisa does make exquisite bread."

Addie pretended not to be offended by the gesture and sat down on the opposite end. The view was picture perfect, with a pond decorated with lily pads floating on the surface and a white bridge that arched over the center of it. None of the scenic beauty mattered as much as the fact that Nora had accepted the treat she had brought out. "So, I know it's not as delicious as cake and ice cream, but now that the secret's out about the horribly innutritious meal you were going to eat, I don't feel quite so badly for ruining your dinner."

"Oh, give me a break." Nora jabbed the roll back onto Addie's napkin and returned to the position of crossing her arms. "I don't eat like that every night."

She found it difficult to hold back the smirk that wanted to form on her lips. "I see, so like what, once a week?"

Nora shot her a disgusted look. "Seriously?"

"Okay, okay, how about once a month?"

"Year. Once a year. On my birthday."

The bite of bread in her mouth got swallowed down with a thick, dry gulp. "I am such a horrible person." Addie closed her eyes and pressed at the stress headache that had instantly started to form between them. "You probably want to fire me now."

"The thought has crossed my mind."

"Let me make this up to you somehow." She felt

her heart pounding with anticipation. She pictured herself spending a night in the woods being eaten alive by mosquitos if she failed to come up with a solution. "Make me do something. Anything you want."

"You are currently under my employ. I can make you do anything I want already."

"Not work related. I mean something ridiculous." She turned to Nora, hoping that her desperate plea would get through to her. "You can come up with something completely crazy, like a dare that I would have to do no matter what. Just name it."

"That is the most absurd thing I've ever heard of. How is that beneficial to me in any way?"

"You're right. It is pointless." Addie stood up. "It's all I could come up with to offer you. I don't have anything else. I sincerely apologize for screwing up your birthday."

She took one final look at Nora. She could have been a subject for a painting with her flawlessly smooth skin, shimmering hair, and soft features. There was a strength in the way she was holding herself, putting up a wall for protection, but Addie could see the shards of pain that she had caused with her careless comments peeking through. She would walk away now and give her time before she made things worse. She hung her head in shame and headed towards the rear entrance of the manor, which was annoyingly simple to see from the outside.

"The pond."

Addie stopped, wondering if she had heard the words correctly, or even at all. She turned slowly to see Nora leaning over the back of the bench with her chin resting on her hands. "What about the pond?"

"Go out onto the bridge and at the center, I want

you to jump in."

Without hesitation, she turned and headed directly for the pond. Her heart pounded as she practically skipped across the lawn. As she passed the bench, she stopped suddenly and set her hands on the arm rest. "You'll have a much better view of the show if you follow me down there."

Nora shrugged her shoulders as if it didn't matter, but she stood up and sauntered along with her anyway. Addie stayed a few steps ahead of her, anxious to prove that she could take direction and leave the personal comments out for the time being.

The narrow wooden bridge was sturdy and looked like it had recently had a fresh coat of white paint applied to it. Addie went right for the rim of the bridge, which was only raised a couple of inches above the rest of it but was barely wide enough for her to stand without her foot hanging over the edge. She made eye contact with Nora, raised her eyebrows up, and made a show of recklessly stumbling on the edge of the bridge. She would pretend to trip and let one leg dangle over the side as if she were about to fall in but catch herself just in time and mock that she was wiping her brow.

Nora followed her every movement with serious brown eyes and a stoic demeanor. Once, Addie caught a slight glimmer of a smile emerging from the corners of her mouth. That tiny bit of joy was fuel enough for the courage she needed for the vile thing she knew was coming next.

Addie crouched down and peered into the murky water below. A plump frog croaked and leapt off a nearby lily pad, splattering a spray of water onto her arm. She smelled it and crinkled her nose at the pungent odor. "So, I'm about to jump into nasty, slimy water, which is most likely filled with leeches, for you."

"It is pretty disgusting, isn't it?"

"If I do this, do you think you could forgive me for the whole dinner incident?" Addie stood and held her hand out to confirm the agreement.

Nora tapped the fingers of her right hand against her thigh and slowly extended her hand out. "I accept your apology."

"And hopefully you'll forgive me for this too." She could feel Nora start to release her grip on their shake. Addie responded quickly by squeezing her hand a little tighter. Then she swung her other arm around Nora's waist. "I'd close your mouth if I were you."

Without a second thought, she pulled Nora's body in close to her own, and dropped over the side of the bridge. The impact with the water was instant since they weren't exceedingly high above it. The liquid was as warm as bath water from the heat of the summer air, yet somewhat refreshing to her hot skin.

Addie emerged mixed in a flurry of tangled limbs with Nora. It was difficult to find footing in the bottom of the mucky pond as her feet sunk into the mud. She pulled up on one foot, the suction almost stealing her sneaker from her, and spread her leg out to get a better balance. She watched with amusement as Nora flailed about as she struggled to stand. Addie finally took pity on her and provided a hand to keep her steady.

Nora coughed out a mouthful of water and glared at Addie through strands of sopping wet hair. "What the hell did you do that for?" She batted away Addie's hand. "You were supposed to jump in, not me!"

"I know, but at the last second I thought it would be kind of fun if we both went in." She started to grin but suppressed it and pressed her lips together when she realized that Nora was still glaring at her.

Suddenly, Nora's mouth opened, and a blood curdling scream shot out of it. She rapidly waved her hands up over the surface of the water and spun from side to side. Her voice shuddered. "Tell me it was you who just rubbed up against my leg."

Addie shook her head slowly. "Nope, not me."

The normally light bronze skin of Nora's face drained of blood so that she was as pale as a marble statue. Addie rushed over to her as fast as the thick mud pulling her under would allow. Despite Nora batting away not only her, but everything in sight, Addie held her breath and ducked under, in order to scoop her up out of water. She had expected some resistance, but it felt comforting to have Nora's arms lock around her neck.

It took a couple of wide, wobbly steps to reach the bridge, every ounce of strength in her muscles, and additional power from an adrenaline rush, to heft Nora up onto it. Addie didn't know how she could possibly muster up the energy to get herself up there also, so she searched around for the closest point to climb up onto the lawn. The thought of sloshing through the slimy undergrowth of the pond with an unknown creature lurking below, and no energy left to do it, was too much to consider. Then, as a complete surprise, a reprieve came in the form of Nora's hand reaching out to her.

Even feeling completely spent, the offering of Nora's help was all the motivation she needed. With their hands locked together, she used her free one to grip the side of the bridge and swung one leg up. For a moment, she teetered precariously from side to side, but Nora made the risky move of releasing her hand to get a hold around her waist. From this position, Addie felt as though she was being rolled like a log until she was safely back on solid ground.

Addie took in a few breaths so heavily that she coughed until her lungs returned to feeling normal. She glanced over at Nora, who was also lying on her back, still recovering herself. "So, I don't suppose you're willing to forgive me for this little mishap along with the others?"

Nora's head turned slowly to the side to face her. She blew a puff of air out to force the clump of wet hair away from her eyes, which had gone from pleasant almond shapes, to two thin slits. The dark of her pupils glared out at her. "My advice to you would be to stop and think before you do or say anything, ever again."

Addie considered throwing herself back into the swampy pond. She wasn't sure if it was more fitting as punishment or to escape how ashamed she felt towards herself. As she worked at forming a new apology, she watched as Nora's mouth dropped open at the sight of something in the water.

They simultaneously flipped over to their stomachs and peered over the edge of the bridge. Nora pointed to a spot in the dark water with a shaky finger, so Addie focused in on that area. Tall blades of grass that grew up out of the water shifted aside as the shadow of something large loomed below the surface. They glanced at each other, wide eyed, and then back at the location where there was movement.

Addie rubbed at the sting in her eyes after refraining from blinking for so long. The reprieve felt so satisfying that had the audible gasp from Nora not alerted her, she would have missed the revealing of the mysterious beast. The shadow made its way to the surface, growing larger as it did, until a head the size of Addie's fist poked out from below. The turtle stretched out its long neck, blinked its eyes, and dove back into the abyss, giving them a glimpse of the back of its shell on its way down. Addie stole a peek at Nora as she watched in awe of the wild creature until it disappeared completely.

Nora released her white-knuckle grip on the bridge. "Can you believe it was just a turtle this whole time?" She broke out into a session of laughter. "All of that for a turtle."

Addie chose not to point out that she had spotted it was a snapping turtle, which could have easily taken off one of their fingers for a snack, and instead she joined Nora in releasing some nervous energy. She laughed until her stomach ached, then looked over at Nora, who was still chuckling, her grin exposing her perfectly lined white teeth. She sighed contentedly, taking Nora's advice not to say or do anything to mess up the joyful moment.

A cool breeze rustled through the trees that lined the end of the yard and as it swept through, it brought goose bumps to their skin. Nora sat up and drew her knees to her chest. She pulled at the loose, wet fabric of her pants that clung to her legs. She rested her chin on her knees, which prompted her nose to wrinkle up in disgust. "Ugh, I smell horrid."

"Did I ruin your clothes?"

"Eh." Nora swiped her hand through the air, dismissing her question. "They can be washed or burned if need be."

"It's difficult to tell whether or not that should be added to the list of ways I destroyed your day."

Nora stood up and rubbed the chill from her bare arms with her hands. "I'm almost too embarrassed to admit that this just may have been the most enjoyable day that I've had in quite a while." She closed her eyes and took in a deep breath. The corners where her lips met curved up slightly into a contented smile. "I'm going in to clean myself up."

Chapter Seven

Just outside the rear entrance to Rosin Manor, Addie squeezed out the excess water from the bottom of her tank top and what she could from her jeans without removing them. She kicked off each of her sneakers and smeared off as much of the mud as she could into the mulch beds. Her socks were just as disgusting, sopping wet and covered in a thick slimy coating. She slipped each one off and wrung them out, adding them to the pile of dirty items. She considered leaving the smelly wet mess outside so that it could dry up and be easier to clean off, but she changed her mind, not wanting to tarnish the pristine backyard.

She gathered up her belongings and tiptoed into the manor. She wasn't intending to be quiet, but it occurred as a result of not wanting to set her entire dirty foot down on the freshly waxed floor. Due to her inadvertent silence, she overheard voices from behind a partially closed door. She paused to listen.

"That woman is a danger to Miss Rosin. I'm going to get rid of Addie before she hurts her any more than she already has." Gregory huffed out and Addie could hear a foot stomp after he spoke.

"Don't be so harsh. Addie hasn't done anything harmful." Lisa's words were scolding, and yet still sounded calming, in a motherly fashion.

"She threw Miss Rosin into the pond!"

"Along with herself, and besides, did you see

how much fun Miss Rosin was having? I haven't seen her laugh in ages."

"If that's what it takes, then we can all take turns throwing Miss Rosin into the pond, shall we?"

Addie chuckled silently to herself and continued down the hallway until she realized that she had no idea where she was headed. Most of the doors were closed and there was no indication what was behind any of them. She made her way to the entryway where the wide staircase stood before her. The urge to follow the staircase up crossed her mind, but the steps were lined with a royal blue carpet that she didn't want to soil with her dirty feet. She stood below the enormous crystal chandelier, then watched as it caught beams of sunlight and spread them like little rainbows across the floor and walls. Fast approaching footsteps from behind brought her out of her trance.

"There you are, Miss Addie." Henry shuffled along so fast to reach her that he sucked in a huge breath. "Oh my, what have they got you doing on your first day? Mucking out the stables?" He waved his hand in front of his nose.

"I could really use a place to clean up."

"Yes, of course, follow me." Henry started towards the staircase.

"Wait, is there another way? I'm disgusting."

He dismissed her concern with a wave of his hand. "Miss Rosin traipses through here in her muddy riding boots all the time. The maid has all sorts of tricks for getting stains out of this rug."

Addie shrugged her shoulders and followed him up the grand staircase. Each step on the thick plush carpet made her sore feet feel as if she were walking on clouds. At the top of the first set, there was a giant mirror with a wide wooden frame. She avoided looking directly at her own reflection and instead focused on the intricately carved wood that depicted Amazon warriors with bows, ready for the hunt.

From here, the staircase broke off in two separate directions. Henry motioned to the left. "As soon as we empty out a room for you, your bedroom will be located down that hall with all the other staff rooms. For the time being, I created a temporary space up this way."

Addie was led to a room with yet another door that took even a grunt on Henry's part to open. As she entered what appeared to be a sitting room furnished with décor from the Victorian era, she let out a little gasp. "This is where I'm staying?"

"I do apologize for not having a proper room available. If this isn't acceptable, I might be able to find other accommodations for you."

"Oh, no, I think you may have misjudged my reaction. This room is absolutely gorgeous."

"The maid, Francine, has laid out some bedding for you to use over on that chair, and the powder room is just across the hall. If you need anything from the kitchen prior to breakfast, feel free to take what you wish. Just please refrain from entering any of the other rooms in this wing of the house."

❧❧❧❧

After soaking in the longest bath she had ever taken, Addie retreated to her makeshift room. Most of the furniture was covered over with large sheets, so she went about the room and pulled some of them off until she found a chaise lounge chair. She spread out the blankets that were left for her and propped a pillow up.

She had thought that it wouldn't take much for her to just close her eyes and be out after the events of the day she had experienced, but instead her mind raced. Conversations repeated themselves and decisions she made replayed, haunting her thoughts. As much as she wanted to blame the sleepless night at having grown accustomed to far more uncomfortable furnishings for so many years, she kept reaching down to pet the empty space where her faithful friend, Buddy, would normally be curled up next to her.

"Ugh." She tossed the blanket aside and started to pace the length of the room. As she went from one end to the other, she uncovered more and more sheets from furniture and decorations.

On one wall was an oil painting of a family. Nora was depicted much younger in the portrait, looking to be around ten. Her father standing behind her had the same black hair and dark eyes. Many of Nora's features mirrored those of her Asian father. Her mother, on the other side of him, with a hand resting proudly on Nora's shoulder, had starkly contrasting characteristics. Her hair was a golden shade of blond and her skin was fair, but what stood out most of all were her bright blue eyes.

For a while, Addie reflected on the picture of the family. She wondered if they posed while the artist created it. She imagined a young Nora complaining about having to sit still for so long and squirming to get free. After creating the scenario in her mind, she decided that they most likely submitted a photo for the artist to recreate it into a work of art.

Removing another furniture covering revealed

an antique music stand with sheet music for a violin resting open on it. "Ah, now I'm on to something." She searched under coffee tables, on shelves, above dressers, and finally was successful when she opened the door of the wardrobe. Propped up in the corner was a hard, black case. She slid it out by the handle but supported it with her other arm, cradling it like a newborn baby.

She carefully set it down on her makeshift bed, and unhinged the three gold latches, each one clanking open. Addie lifted the cover, but before examining it any further, she closed her eyes and inhaled the exquisite smell of old wood, mixed with varnish. Delicately lifting the instrument out of its case, she could already hear the thin hollow wood resonating in her hands, begging to sing out. Next, she removed the bow and tightened the horse hairs until they were at just the right tension. Luckily, the pocket in the case had a well-worn block of rosin hidden in it, which she applied in long strokes to the bow.

Each one of the strings she plucked were in desperate need to be tuned and could have stood to be replaced all together, but they would have to do for now. She rested the instrument under her chin and put the bow in position to begin playing. Lots of options came to mind, but when the muscle memory of her fingers hit the strings, it was one of the classics that automatically emerged.

At first, she attempted to play quietly, barely applying any pressure to the bow against the strings, but as the song progressed, the muted sound rapidly increased to full volume. For a time, she kept a nervous watch for someone to complain about the noise level, but that unease faded when she convinced herself that the walls surely must be as thick as the doors.

Without proper callouses built up, the pads of her fingers stung, but she pushed through the pain. The longer she played, the slower the speed of transitioning from one note to the next became, but she played on. As time progressed, she chose slower songs, drawing out the notes to make each one sound like the melody of a lullaby. The muscles in her arms spasmed. She fought through the last few measures of the tune before setting the instrument in her lap. Her eyes felt heavy and started to close, but the door opening startled her awake.

Nora stepped into the room with a wilted posture. Her look was blank, and her eyes darted around the room as if she were looking for answers. She stopped when she caught sight of the violin. "It was you who was playing just now."

"Yes, I'm sorry if I woke you."

Nora shook her head. "Don't worry, I wasn't sleeping." She looked around the room again. "Henry asked me about a room for you. I told him anywhere was fine for a night or two. I just didn't think he would put you *here*."

"I don't mind it. It's a gorgeous room."

"That's not what I mean." Nora's words came out blunt and fast.

Addie searched her foggy mind. "Oh, it's like the table thing. Henry mentioned that the staff quarters are on the opposite side of the manor. I can go find somewhere else to crash for the night on the other side, if you'd like."

"No, it's fine." She waved off Addie's offer to move. Her eyes focused in on the violin again and she moved in closer to where it was located on her lap. She bent down and came in hesitantly, but then refrained at the last second. "Could you just put that back in the case and return it to the wardrobe, please?"

"Yes, of course. I just saw the sheet music on the stand, and it's been so long since I've last played."

"You play beautifully." Nora bit at the corner of her lower lip. "It's just that, well, this particular violin is special."

"I agree. The sound on this one is superb." Addie lifted it to inspect the label inside the body of the instrument. Instead of the typical paper label, there were a series of intersecting lines in the fibers that were visible. She couldn't translate what was written, but she recognized that it was in the Latin language. She felt the tiny gasp of air escape from her mouth. The violin that she was playing with such vigor minutes earlier, she now held as if it would blow away like ashes if she moved the wrong way. "Is this a Stradivarius?"

"Yes, it is, but I meant that it's special because it used to belong to my mother, and it has been in my family for generations." Nora bobbed her head along to the second half of her explanation as if it were verbatim ingrained in her over time.

"Hmm, yes, a family heirloom." What she failed to mention was that the last violin found by the same luthier sold for millions. Addie gingerly placed the violin back in its case and closed the lid, holding her breath the entire time. "I promise that I will not only return it back safely but put everything in this room just as I found it."

"Don't bother. Francine comes in regularly to dust and wash the sheets." Nora's eyes scanned the room. "I don't suppose there's much luggage in that one little bag of yours?"

In all the worry about potentially committing yet another wrong-doing, Addie had overlooked that she was wearing nothing but a single white towel, wrapped around her body. "I came with only the clothes on my back."

"The ones that are a wet, muddy mess now." Nora stepped to the doorway and flagged Addie over. "Come with me."

The hardwood floors were chilly on Addie's bare feet as she padded along behind Nora through another Victorian themed room fit for royalty. The king-sized bed appeared to be minuscule in relation to the spacious room. They passed through with enough speed that it was evident to Addie that this was not a sightseeing tour, despite her urge to want to get a closer look at some of the tapestries hanging on the walls.

She followed Nora to the far end of the bedroom and waited as she slid open one side of a double wide door and flipped a switch just inside it. A row of lights flickered to life, illuminating the long, wide closet. Addie had seen some large closets before, but this one was comparable to the size of studio apartments in the city.

Nora continued to the back section of the closet, where she stopped and turned around. She swept her hands in a motion that encompassed the length of her body. "I unfortunately got my height from my mother, which is why I can't share any of my own clothes with you. That also leaves out this entire side of the closet." She turned away from the side containing the more feminine selection of clothes to face the more masculine side. "You seem to be more of my father's height, and though it won't be a perfect fit, at least your legs won't be exposed up to your calves."

Addie reached for a tag dangling from the sleeve of a shirt and then another right next to it. "These are all brand new."

"Yes, mostly everything in this back section had been purchased but not worn yet. I'd prefer that you only wear the new items." Nora passed by Addie. "This is only temporary until we order you exactly what you want."

Addie spun around to the other side of the closet, reached for a bright pink velour robe, and made sure there was a tag attached. She turned her back to Nora, then released the knot on her towel. The second it fell to her feet she whipped the robe around herself in a flashy show as if it were a superhero cape. "This will do fine. Thank you."

Nora's eyes were aimed in her direction, and her cheeks had blushed to a shade matching the robe before she quickly turned away. "I'll see you in the morning. Please turn off the light when you are finished." Without looking back, she waved over her shoulder and swiftly retreated.

Alone with a new wardrobe to pick through, Addie tried on a few outfits and piled them neatly to bring back with her. She opened a couple of shoe boxes in the long shot that they might have a similar shoe size, and in doing so, came across a metal box at the bottom of the pile. Inside was a pistol.

Due to her boss' obsession with flashing his gun to show how powerful he was, it wasn't too shocking for Addie to unveil the weapon. This one was heavily adorned with jewels on the grip and appeared to be old enough that it most likely was another piece in Mr.

Rosin's exquisite collection. He probably just kept it hidden in the closet because it was a working weapon in a family home. She closed the lid on the metal box and slid it back where she found it.

The shiny jewels on the gun did spark her interest, though, in what might be located inside the jewelry box nestled within Mrs. Rosin's accessory section of the closet. She pulled both sides of the cabinet open at the same time, revealing a glimmering selection of necklaces each hanging on its own hook. There were a variety of colors from different stones, but there were clear favorites in sapphires, rubies, and diamonds, given there were more compared to the other precious stone types.

Moving down to the drawers on the bottom of the cabinet, she slid out the first one to find a selection of earrings. Each pair was placed in perfect little grids to separate them from becoming tangled together. The next drawer was bracelets, but mostly simple designs made from metals that were difficult to determine. Again, there was an air of disappointment when she found a drawer full of watches, each one with a band wrapped around a velvet pedestal display.

Her hand hovered over the handle of the final drawer just long enough for a silent plea to cross her mind. "Oh yeah." She covered her mouth with her hand to hold back the excitement as the sparkles from the rings danced under the fluorescent bulb in the closet. This one was a welcomed mess that needed to be sifted through to reach the wooden base. She picked up one after another to check the diamonds, and by only using sight as a judge, and a simple breath of hot air on the surface, she was quite sure that they were all real.

It was after coming across a brilliant sapphire which appeared to be multiple carats in size, that she second guessed her ability to determine a fake. "You must just be costume jewelry, right?" She twirled the ring around while examining the craftsmanship of the setting. She remembered where she was. The amount of money spent on artwork, furniture, and landscaping had proven that this quite possibly was indeed a quality gemstone.

"You are my ticket to getting Buddy back." She planted a tiny kiss on the blue stone before slipping it into the pocket of the robe.

Chapter Eight

Addie entered the kitchen the next morning, pushing open the door with a newly found confidence after practicing on the one to her bedroom until she got the hang of it. There were a few people around the table, but some were missing from the group at dinner the previous evening.

"Good morning, dear. I've got pancakes, bacon, and fresh fruit on the table. Oh, and let me know if the syrup has cooled off so I can reheat it for you." Lisa started to squeeze a fresh orange into a carafe.

"Sounds great. I'm starving." Addie had been headed to the table but stopped short when she noticed the covered tray on the table. "Do you want me to take this into the dining room for Nora?"

"No need, it's already empty. Nora rises early every morning and heads off to the stables for a ride."

"Hmm, stables, okay." Addie meandered over to the table. She could feel Gregory's eyes staring her down, but she focused on some plump blueberries to pop in her mouth.

"You were explicitly told not to wander in that wing of the manor, other than your assigned quarters." Gregory pushed his chair out and stood. "I'd recognize the designer of those pants anywhere. You've taken them from Mr. Rosin's closet."

Addie looked down at her choice of pinstripe suit pants and a white shirt with short sleeves. "Yes, they are from his wardrobe." She tossed a piece of melon into the air and caught it in her mouth.

"Then I have no choice but to tell Miss Rosin that you have violated the rules."

"If that's what you feel you must do, then by all means, go ahead." She stopped to eat a couple of raspberries. "It would be wrong of me, though, not to inform you that Nora was the one who offered these clothes to me when mine got wet."

Gregory did not respond, but he did emit a low, guttural growl that was probably difficult for anyone any farther away to pick up on. He sat back down, shifted awkwardly in his seat, and folded his arms gruffly.

As entertaining as Addie thought it might be to watch a grown man stave off a temper tantrum, she had other plans. The stack of fluffy pancakes piled high in the center of the table looked too good to pass up on, so she removed two from the top of the stack. She rolled each one up, dipped the ends in syrup, and headed towards the kitchen door. "If anyone needs me, I'll be out at the stables."

Gregory's voice was so loud that it was obvious that he intended for her to overhear. "Well, isn't she charming?"

She raised up one of the pancake rolls, dripping in syrup, to toast his insult. "Cheers to that." She took a bite off the end, closed her eyes, and savored the taste. "Lisa, these taste heavenly."

The newly found rear exit to the manor made access to the backyard so much quicker, but then there was the matter of finding the stables on the sprawling grounds that seemed to spread out as far as her eyes could see in either direction. It took her a few failed attempts at entering storage barns, garden sheds, and garages, before she found hope in a large barn with several bales of hay stacked outside of it. One side of the double barn doors was open, so she wandered in.

The front section of the barn was wide open. To the left was an array of riding equipment hanging on the walls. Rows of saddles, helmets, straps, and blankets filled the space up to the rafters. To the right were barrels overflowing with pellets, shovels, brushes, and other grooming supplies. Where this section ended was about as far as the natural light entering through the door could reach. Beyond that, the walkway through the center of the barn narrowed where it was sectioned off for each of the separate stalls.

Addie took a few slow steps and blinked her eyes, trying to adjust to the darkness. "Is there anyone in here?" She could feel her voice shake and was glad that no one answered her. The sound of shuffling and movement came from farther back, so she continued forward but got disoriented in her direction due to her lack of vision. A booming thump stopped her in her tracks, and she felt a burst of hot air blow across the top of her head.

In a panic, she rushed towards the lit area of the barn. Until now, she hadn't realized just how far back she had wandered, but on a hay covered floor with low visibility, the end seemed miles away. A loud screech behind her caused Addie to look back as the door on the opposite end of the barn rolled open, illuminating the areas that weren't visible before.

She let out a sigh of relief at the safety of not being in unfamiliar territory in the dark, but mistakenly took a step backwards in the process. Something reached around and touched the side of her face. She jerked out of the way and turned to see a horse's head extending out over the gate of its stall. "Ugh, gross." She wiped the wet spot off her cheek with the back of her hand.

"Don't worry. They won't harm you." The woman with the long blond hair came through the barn, leading a horse beside her. She wiped her hand off on her shirt and held it out. "I didn't get the opportunity to formally introduce myself at dinner last night. I'm Ruth."

Addie rubbed her dirty fingers against the palm of her hand to remove the grime but didn't offer to shake. "I'm slathered in horse spit, but it's nice to meet you."

"Trust me, there is rarely a time when I'm not covered in something nasty that came from one of these guys." She swept her hand to point out the stalls along both sides of the barn, many of which had heads hanging out over the tops of them. Ruth pulled the latch on an empty stall and guided the horse in. "I can teach you to ride so you won't be so afraid."

"I'm good, thanks, and I'm not afraid of horses." Addie let out a sigh of relief that the horse was safely contained away from her. "How long have you been working here?"

"When Miss Rosin started high school, I was part of her private teaching staff for math and science. I stayed on until she finished school and then stayed to tend to the horses."

"Then you haven't left Rosin Manor in years."

"Seven. I've personally lost track, but there are the usual complainers who consistently keep reminding everyone of how long it's been."

"It must be difficult. I mean, this place is gorgeous beyond measure, but that has to get old eventually."

"The way I look at it is that this situation is temporary. Miss Rosin has a fear of the outside world. I believe that eventually she can and will be healed from her agoraphobia and we can go back to living normal lives. Until then, we all have to do our part for her and the manor."

"She's lucky to have so many people willing to sacrifice their freedom to cater to her mental illness." Addie cringed, unaware if she was speaking too openly about someone she hardly knew with a person who clearly adored her.

"Has anyone told you the reason why she doesn't leave the manor?"

Addie shook her head and pushed together a pile of sawdust with the side of the borrowed sneaker, which was a size too large for her, but suitable until hers dried. "I figure that if Nora wants me to know, then she'll tell me when she's ready to."

"Most people, given the opportunity, would choose gossip over hearing it directly from the person affected." Ruth's eyes bore into her with a hard stare, but then shifted to vacant, as if she were trying to work something out in her head. "You could be the key to changing things here."

"How?"

"We have all given in to her fears out of an obligation to her and her family. Maybe all it takes is an outsider to break her phobia."

"I'm here to fix my own problems, not yours."

"Fine, just promise me that if you don't plan on sticking around, you won't let Miss Rosin get attached to you. She's still fragile and losing someone else would be devastating to her."

"You don't have to worry about that. I'm not the kind of person people get attached to."

Addie rushed out of the barn. She didn't know what was worse, the giant hovering horses, or the pressure to become some sort of savior to a group of people she hardly knew and a place she planned on leaving behind in a week.

The idea of only one week to get Buddy back began to loom over her. She had started to come up with a plan, but she needed to talk to Mason to see if he would be on board with her. The minutes on the burner phone that he had provided her with to conduct dealer business had long since run out for the month, and she had no money to purchase more. There was only one way she knew of to contact him, so she went to the only phone she had seen in the manor.

She knocked on Gregory's office door, loud enough for him to hear if he were inside, but quiet enough not to draw attention if it were empty. Luckily, there was no answer, so she let herself in and went over to the landline phone she had noticed in there the day before. She chose the number to one of Mason's phones that he only gave out to clients because the chances of him answering a strange number on his personal phone were next to none.

"Sup?" Mason's voice sounded groggy even through one partial word.

"Hey, it's me, Add."

"Do you have my money?"

She cupped her hand around the mouthpiece of the phone and whispered, "I have a ring. The stone on it is worth even more than I owe you. You can have it and keep the extra money that I know you can get for it."

"I told you I want cash. I don't run a fucking pawn shop."

"Fine. I'll get you the money. How is Buddy doing?"

"Stop worrying about the damn pooch and get me my money!"

The door to the office creaked open and Addie almost dropped the handset as she stumbled to hang it up as fast as possible.

There was rapid clicking of shoes on the hardwood floor and Gregory was standing with his hands on his hips, staring her down. "What are you doing behind my desk?"

"My cellphone isn't working. I had to contact my..." She tried to inconspicuously search the room for an answer, while pretending to need to remove something stuck in her tooth. "Dentist. I had to cancel my appointment, which was scheduled before I found out that I would be here indefinitely."

He glowered at her. "If that unlikely story is true, then you will be assured to know that we have a dentist come on site every six months for regular cleanings and whatever dental work you need done."

"Good to know."

"I will also order you a new cellphone, so you won't need to meddle in my office space."

Embarrassed that she was absentmindedly still occupying the space behind his desk, Addie side stepped her way out from behind it, mindful not to disturb any of the stacks of paperwork on her way by. "A phone would be much appreciated."

"If you are finished with your personal calls, I

have a project for you."

"Project?"

"Yes, or a job, if you prefer. You do *work* here, if you recall."

She had preferred the idea that it might possibly be Nora who was delegating her chores out to her, but it made sense that it would be the Rosin Manor manager who had the authority to do so. She promptly saluted him. "Ready for your orders, boss."

Gregory blew past her to a safe in the corner of the room. He glanced over his shoulder and flashed her a warning look. Addie pretended to be disinterested in watching him enter the safe's code, but she really had no interest in it anyway. It was the contents inside that she nonchalantly worked at getting a view of. It was difficult to see around the protective wall that he placed between her line of sight and the inside of the safe, but just as she had expected, he emerged with a small stack of cash in his hand.

"A delivery truck should be arriving shortly. Tip the driver with this." He handed the bills to Addie. "Our shipments vary, but most are labeled for who they belong to. Just do your best to sort them to the right places in the manor."

Chapter Nine

Addie set down the final box from the shipment in which she had spent the last hour running around to various parts of the manor to deliver. The process would have probably gone much faster had she been better informed of the layout of Rosin Manor. A part of her thought that it might be a fun task in the future once she had memorized every location, but she promptly shut down the idea when she remembered how her time spent at the manor would be short lived. She waited until last to bring out the one that had to go all the way out to the stables. The excuse she had told herself was the distance was the farthest point she had to travel to, but as a horse bucked and neighed in a stall, she realized what she was really avoiding. She pushed the box aside and retreated out of the barn so quickly that she had to dodge Nora to avoid slamming into her.

"Where are you headed off to in such a rush?" Nora stood with her arms crossed and yet the smirk across her lips gave away that she might be in a playful mood.

"I was thinking about taking a dip in the pond again this morning and I was wondering if you wanted to join me?"

Nora let out a soft, partly suppressed laugh. "Once was plenty enough for me."

"I figured."

They both stood with an awkward silence between them. Addie tried to indiscreetly stare at how the tight, tan leggings showed off the curves of Nora's thighs. Below that, they flowed into the tall leather boots that contoured perfectly to her calves. She changed her focus to the top half, where she followed each one of the gold buttons of Nora's navy-blue riding coat up to where it changed over to a white collared shirt that fit snug around her neck.

"So, rumor has it you're afraid of horses."

Addie felt her jaw drop open. "I am so *not* afraid of horses."

A snicker made Nora's shoulder's bounce. "Ruth said that you just about leapt out of your own skin when a horse moved in a stall."

"It was dark, and I wasn't expecting it."

"She also said you looked like you were going to be sick when she offered to teach you to ride."

"Okay, I'll admit that they creep me out, but I had a bad experience with a horse when I was a kid."

"If you've ridden before, then I bet all it would take is for you to get back up on one. If you just try, maybe it will be different for you. I have an old sweet mare who takes everything slow. We could ride together."

In that moment, seeing Nora flash a warm and eager smile, Addie probably would have done anything she asked. It occurred to her, though, that if she was able to help change things at Rosin Manor, then she might possibly be able to pull off both getting Buddy back, and having a place with a good job to return to. "How about if we make a little deal? I'll ride a horse if you do something that scares you."

"I'm guessing you already have something in

mind?"

She didn't, but there were a bunch of flier advertisements still fresh in her mind from yesterday. "There is a show tomorrow night. The Woo Girls are playing at a venue in the city. I'd love to see their gig with you."

Nora stared past her with a vacant expression. Addie repeated what she just suggested to her in her head and wondered if it was too much to ask for. The woman hasn't left her property in seven years and now she may have just completely insulted her by thinking that she would attend a major crowded event far from home.

"So, let me be clear on this. You'll ride on a horse with me and in exchange I have to go to a Woo Girls show with you tomorrow night?"

Addie swallowed an audible gulp. "Uh huh." She waited for the barrage of reasons why she was so insensitive to follow.

"It's a deal but only on one more condition."

"I'm listening."

"We will have dinner together here before the show."

"You drive a hard bargain, but you have yourself a deal." Addie stuck out her pinky finger and winked at her.

Nora stared curiously at the gesture. "I haven't seen one of those since childhood, or in film."

"A pinky promise?"

"Yes. That seems to be an odd way for adults to agree upon something."

"Well, the last time we shook, I pulled you into the pond with me, so I figured this might be a fresh start to trusting me."

"You have a valid point." Nora curved her finger and intertwined it in a lock with hers. "Now that we are settled, let's get started with that ride."

"Right now?"

"My riding clothes are still on. This is the perfect time to go." Nora stepped in closer to Addie and gave the top of her arm a little squeeze. "Unless it's too scary for you. We can always call the deal off."

"Ha! I was about to offer the same to you, but you'll have to decide fast, because I'm about ready to hop on a horse right now." Addie looked around, pretending that she was disappointed that there wasn't one in the vicinity.

Nora raised her arm and waved her fingers.

Responding to the beckoning, Ruth emerged from the barn with a horse in tow. "I couldn't help but overhear that you wanted to ride." She let the helmet in her hand dangle by the strap, using a single finger, and held it out to Addie.

For a moment, Addie doubted her decision to help create change at Rosin Manor. She questioned whether it would be beneficial to her in the long run, or if there just wasn't enough time for that. If that was the case, then she was just wasting her time at her own expense, doing one of the things she feared the most. As she reached for the helmet, though, Ruth leaned in and Addie caught the glimmer of tears in her eyes. She also caught the nod of appreciation bestowed upon her, and with that, she reluctantly took the helmet and plopped it on her head.

Nora took the reins from Ruth and guided the horse closer to Addie. "This sweet old girl is Dot." She soothed the palm of her hand up the ridge of the horse's nose.

Addie stepped out of the path of the horse, even though she wasn't moving. "Heh, no need for introductions. This is going to be a one-time thing between us, not a lifelong friendship."

"I can respect that." Nora slid the toe of her boot into a stirrup and pushed up to swing her leg over the saddle. She shimmied forward and held her hand out to Addie; simultaneously, Ruth came from behind and set a step stool down behind her.

"Seriously, ladies, just because I'm not a fan of horses does not mean that I'm incapable of getting up on one." Addie gripped onto the rear of the saddle and hoisted herself up using the stirrup.

Nora arched her head over her shoulder. "Look at you, cowgirl. Does that mean you're too tough to hang on for the ride?"

She could feel Nora's hips rock forward and down in the saddle, urging the horse to move. Addie clutched onto the rear of the saddle behind her with two hands to steady herself. "You did mention that she's old and slow, right?"

"We can move at a snail's pace if that's the speed you feel comfortable riding at."

"To get the full experience of taking in the sights of Rosin Manor's grounds, I'm thinking that a relaxing sort of *crawl* would be best." Addie risked removing one of her hands from the saddle to make a slow movement of two fingers walking over Nora's shoulder. "Otherwise, without leaving the grounds, we will have quite a short ride."

"Fortunately for us, I own hundreds upon hundreds of acres of land. Ruth spends much of her days out breaking new trails for us to ride on."

Addie didn't attempt to suppress her groan.

"Lucky us."

"I did just get a vigorous canter in though, so a leisurely trot sounds like a perfect speed."

She let out a breath she had been holding in and allowed her stiff posture to relax into the confines of the space available on the shared saddle. Addie put in motion a plan to stay on guard for potential dangers but promised herself she would make every effort to not let her fears overcome her. As they traversed the outskirts of the manor's backyard, this method worked for the most part.

The horse stopped often to graze on the lush green grass, giving her a chance to readjust her tight muscles from clutching so tightly. The transportation, while nerve wracking, provided a great way to see all the small buildings on the property without having to get to them on foot. Addie created a map in her mind of how to get back to certain places if there were any more shipments which she might be responsible for that week.

The rhythmic motion of the horse's gait beneath her lulled her into a trance, which put her at ease enough that she hadn't noticed they had entered the forested area at the rear of the yard. The dim light from the overhanging trees above the narrow path brought it to her attention that they were in new territory. It was starkly different from the wide-open grassy lawn which felt like a safe and cushioned place to land in a fall. She looked down at the hard-packed dirt path, littered with branches, and lined with root systems extending out from tree trunks to create a natural obstacle course.

Addie could feel the beads of sweat dripping from her forehead down to her ears, but she didn't dare let go of the saddle to wipe them away. She closed her eyes and tried to imagine that they were back in a more open area. As her heart rate   slowed and her breathing became more controlled, she finally felt at ease. It was an odd sensation, though, because she was so calm that she could no longer feel any movement, the sun was warm against her face as if the shadows were gone, and she could hear the tranquil babble of running water surrounding her. Confused, she couldn't help but to leave behind her peaceful escape of serenity to see what was happening. She cracked open her eyes ever so slightly to start but was startled back to reality as just a few inches away, there was another pair staring back at her.

"Are you okay?" Nora twisted the leather strap of the reign up around her hand.

Addie observed her surroundings. They had come to a stop in a wide opening where the sun beamed down, and a flowing stream crossed in front of them. "All things considered; I'm doing okay."

"You had your eyes closed for quite a while."

"Uh huh." She held her hands up about an inch apart from one another. "Tighter spaces when I'm not on my own two feet are easier to deal with when I can't see anything."

"Do you want to get off and take a break for a while?" Nora pressed the back of her hand to Addie's forehead. "You could splash some cool water on your face."

"How far are we from the barn?"

"Probably close to a mile from here."

"We've seriously gone *that* far already?" Addie rubbed at the pressure building between her eyes. "If I get off now, then I'll never want to get up again, and that is quite a hike back."

"You should have told me when it got too scary for you. I would have turned around right away." Nora spun so that she was facing in the right direction again and reached behind herself with both hands.

At first Addie started to panic that Nora had set the reigns down, but then she figured out that it was so that she could reach out for her. Addie made her hands available for whatever it was that Nora wanted, so that she could get back in control of the horse faster. Nora grasped around her wrists and pulled Addie's arms around her waist. "This isn't necessary. I did perfectly fine holding onto the saddle this entire ride so far. I don't need to lean on you for support."

Nora clasped onto her thighs and prompted her to shimmy up closer so that her entire body was pressed against hers. "You may think that the death grip you've been using on the saddle is working for you, but your muscles will thank you tonight for giving them a break now."

As difficult as it was to accept that her method of not showing weakness was not helping towards overcoming her fears, it felt relieving to give in to the support of someone who cared. "I do agree this position feels less like my arms are on fire."

"Then I don't suppose you'd be willing to consider that we could go just a tad bit faster?"

"I was about to see what your thoughts were on kicking things down a notch."

"Seriously, if we go any slower, Dot is going to fall asleep. Besides, it would get us back to the barn and off the horse that much sooner."

"No need to convince me any further, go for it." Addie tugged on the lapel of Nora's riding coat.

"*Safely*, that is."

They turned around precariously in the stream and Addie was sure that with every step, the horse would lose its footing on the slippery rocks below the water's surface. Even if she caught herself closing her eyes and wincing in fear, she found that she was also impressed at Nora's expert handling skills. Despite her nerves being rattled, she was thankful to be in such capable hands. Once they returned to the trail, though, it didn't take much time before they emerged out from the jumbled forest to the pristine order of the yard. The thought of having some give offered from the lawn seemed to be a better alternative to the array of tree trunks that she risked being flung at.

"Just a little farther now." Nora gave her hand a light squeeze. "Are you still with me?"

"We made a deal. It would be a shame to back out this late."

Nora directed Dot towards the barn, within sight, but still in the distance. Addie could tell that she was holding the horse back from going at her usual pace. The thought of going any faster made her shudder, but she did think that it would be wonderful to watch Nora ride sometime in the future when she could do it as a spectator and not a participant. She pictured Nora being able to move at whatever speed suited her, uninhibited by a passenger with a paralyzing fear.

Addie had gotten so caught up in how horrible of an experience the ride was for herself that she hadn't thought of until now how difficult it would be for Nora when it came time to fulfill her end of the deal. The ability to avoid horses was completely feasible, especially for Addie living in the city. The concept of never leaving her property in seven years was something that Nora had to struggle with every moment of her life. She leaned in closer to Nora's ear. "I'm going to close my eyes and hold on tighter. Let's try going slightly faster."

"Are you sure?"

Addie squeezed her eyes shut and pressed her face into the crook of Nora's neck. "Uh huh, but make it happen before I change my mind."

Without the ability to see, by choice, she relied on her other senses to determine what the ride was like. At first, there was a gradual increase of movement below her. She locked her hands together around Nora's waist. Then, the wind whipped up the hair hanging out of the base of Nora's helmet and swept it around Addie's face, which was still sheltered against her back.

All her senses flashed warnings that she was going much faster than she had intended when she gave the go ahead to Nora. She searched for an excuse as to why they needed to slow down again, but when she tried to speak, a garbled mess that was too muffled to be heard or understood came out. Instead, she opted for a signal that would get her attention and hopefully prompt her to slow.

She unclasped one of her hands from the other, and while maintaining her firm grip around Nora's waist, she began rapidly tapping her hand. She wasn't sure if her message was being received, until much to her relief, the horse came to a halt. She cracked open her eyes and peeled her face off Nora's back. She could feel her hand frantically still rapping against Nora, so she eased out of the embarrassment of it by pretending that she was straightening out the lapel of her riding coat from the wrinkles created by their embrace.

Just when she thought that she had escaped complete ridicule for her irrational behavior, she heard clapping and cheers of congratulations from below her. Addie checked her surroundings and was mortified to see that they had made it back to the barn. Not only was Ruth joyously celebrating their return, but Henry had joined her with what looked like a tray of refreshments.

Ruth had prepared an easy exit to dismount from the horse onto a bale of hay that they had pulled up next to. Addie decided that this was not the time to refuse the convenient method over her stubborn need to do things her way. Whatever would get her off the horse the swiftest way possible was what mattered. She used the stirrup and swung her leg over, practically allowing herself to fall onto the block of hay with a thud. If she didn't have an audience with all eyes on her, she imagined that she might have stayed laying in that same spot for a while longer, but instead, she popped up to a sitting position and let her legs dangle over the edge of the bale. Addie wouldn't have minded Nora's company, but much to her dismay, Ruth started in with the clapping again and Henry might have joined in had his hands been free from the tray he was carrying.

"You did great out there." Ruth added a whistle to her celebratory repertoire.

"Calm down, cheerleader, all I did was hold on for dear life while Nora did all the work."

Nora dismounted from the horse, looped the reigns around a hook attached to the barn, and joined the circle they had formed. "I think what Ruth means is that you went from being freaked out by being in the presence of a horse to going on a ride on one, regardless of who was in control."

"Yes, we are all very proud of you, Miss Addie." Henry held out the silver tray so that it was in reach of her. "Have a refreshment in honor of your success."

The platter had a variety of cupcakes perfectly lined along the outer rim. She plucked one up and examined the design in the frosting. When she turned it in just the right direction, it was a profile of a horse's head outlined by a carved piece of fondue and filled in with brightly colored sprinkles. A single miniature chocolate chip created the eye. She pulled down the paper liner that was printed with little bursts of fireworks and took a bite.

A sweet explosion attacked her taste buds with a delightful blend of sugar, butter, and vanilla frosting. It was just the treat that she needed after putting her body through a vigorous period of fear and stress. Once past the topping, she hit the cake mixture at the base of the cupcake, which was still warm from the oven. "How did Lisa even accomplish pulling off baking these in the short time that we were gone for?"

"News travels fast in this place." Nora took a cupcake for herself. "And I'm certain that Lisa must have her most loved baked goods premixed so that she's ready for occasions such as this."

"Hopefully news travels just as fast that I've conquered my fear." Addie narrowed her eyes in Ruth's direction and licked off a dab of frosting that had fallen onto her finger. "Although, it might have been worth the humiliation for this tasty treat."

Ruth waved away the offer when Henry made the rounds to her. "You may find the treats to die for in the beginning, but your waistline will soon regret the indulgence." She rubbed at her stomach and scrunched up her face. "If you really want to gain some reputation of being over your fear, you could help me muck out the stables."

Addie popped the last bite of cupcake into her mouth and covered her hand in front of it while she chewed. "While that sounds like fun and all, the one thing that's worse than a horse is the stuff that comes out of them." She crinkled up her nose for effect. "What really matters is that since you're passing, there's seconds for me." She homed in on the closest baked good on the platter until she noticed the tall glasses in the center. "What's in the flutes?"

"Sparkling seltzer on this side and champagne on the other." Henry drew an invisible line dividing the two choices of beverages with his white gloved hand.

A darting glance around the circle showed that all eyes were on her, so Addie pulled up one of the tall glasses bubbling with the sparkling water, cautious not to bump the delicate crystal of the others surrounding it. She took a long sip from the glass and gulped it down. "Mm, refreshing."

"Miss, would you mind taking one from the other side too please? The tray is off balance and I wouldn't want to drop it on the way back to the kitchen." Henry flashed her a wink.

She obliged by taking one from the champagne side. "Well, we wouldn't want that now, would we?" Addie held the glass up in a silent toast and nodded her head to the others before downing the bubbly beverage. As the flavorful liquid slid down her throat, she was reminded that the only indulgent gift from her other boss had been a craft beer that he was too full to finish off from the case. Great food aside, she was beginning to form a list of reasons why it would be difficult to leave Rosin Manor when the time came.

Chapter Ten

One by one, the others had dismissed themselves from their little gathering and Addie found herself alone, still perched up on the haystack. Although she had never had an actual job due to her time in college followed by an abrupt transition to homelessness, she knew that the situation at Rosin Manor was a strange one compared to a traditional workplace. There was an expectation of it to be more rigid than working illegally for a drug dealer as far as tasks, although this seemed to be a generally relaxed environment to the point in which she questioned if she was supposed to be doing something that she wasn't aware of.

She lowered herself off the hay bale and peered into the entryway of the barn door, where Ruth was sorting through the box that she had dropped off earlier. "Is there some sort of employee handbook that I haven't been given that outlines what I should be doing around here?"

"The idea of one might sound handy for you now because you seem a little lost. What you will soon come to find is that the glorious thing about living and working here is the lack of structure."

"I don't see a *lack* of anything here."

Ruth tossed the empty cardboard box into a recycling bin. "Tell me, what do you see?"

"Everything appears to run smoothly and work

together like the gears on a well-oiled machine. It seems like everyone runs around like robots and is instantly there when something is needed. I just want to know my role so that I can be a robot like the rest of you."

Ruth laughed and shook her head. "You have to think of this place like a family running a household. There are certain things that must be done daily to keep a property this large maintained. Each person has their own strengths and likes that they prefer to contribute to do their part here. As time goes on and you see what sorts of things we do on a regular basis, you will find your niche."

"Does the speed come with repetition?"

"That and the fact that when you are done with your job, you can literally do whatever you please. You are on duty per se at all hours of the day, but that gives you time to slack off if there isn't something else that should be done. People have learned to finish a task promptly and get to relaxing just as fast."

"Ah, now I get it." Addie tapped her finger to her head. "Work efficiently and fast, then play or relax sooner and longer."

"Precisely. That is the secret to being a robot, as you like to call us."

"I can get on board with that, but do I have to take direction from Gregory for everything?" Addie started another little sawdust mount between her feet.

"Not a fan, huh?" A grimace spread across Ruth's face. "Don't worry, none of us are, but you'll get used to dealing with his mood swings. Unfortunately, he does know all the details on things like shipments, manor tours, and planning anything to do with the outside world coming to us, so he tends to delegate jobs out. The good thing is that Miss Rosin can override anything he says. If she asks something of you, drop everything else and attend to her needs."

"Hopefully, that will happen often in my case."

"Lucky for you, you're new here. She will most likely be looking for opportunities to spend time with you."

"I'm sure, since you overheard the conversation about our deal, that you know her end of it is to go to the show with me tomorrow night."

"I did." Ruth picked up a saddle blanket and shook the dust from it. "All I ask is that you aren't too hard on her if tomorrow evening doesn't go quite as you're expecting it to."

"Is there something you know about that you're not telling me?"

Ruth shook her head. "You have to understand that we have all tried, often multiple times, over the past seven years to get Miss Rosin to leave the grounds. Every attempt has been unsuccessful."

"The difference between those times and now is that, like you said before, I'm new. Maybe all it takes is someone from the outside to change her perspective on things." Addie started to back out of the barn. Deep down, she knew the positive outlook of the situation in which she let Ruth believe she had was not probable. There was no way that Nora would make such a drastic change in the short timeframe that she had. The means to fix her other problem were already found in the jewelry she had taken. There was no point in sticking around to help someone who might be planning to fool her in a promise that was made between them.

"Before you go, could you do me a favor and

return this to the library for me?" Ruth pulled a book from a nearby shelf and held it out to Addie.

Addie fretted over whether she had just shared her thoughts of leaving aloud, but decided that, even though she hadn't, Ruth was the one who had urged her to leave on two other occasions, if her intentions were not in Nora's best interest. "Yeah, no problem. I assume the library is in the main building?"

"Yes, and since it sounds like you haven't been there yet, you're in for a treat, especially if you enjoy literature."

Addie used the book to wave a farewell to Ruth as she headed back to the manor. She began to plan out where it might be located given the areas in which she had already explored versus the spaces available that would fit a library. Even given the fact that she still had not seen many of the rooms, according to Ruth's description, she figured that it must be large.

From her exterior location, she had a great vantage point of the layout. One spot on other occasions had caught her eye from both the front and rear of Rosin Manor's grounds. It was unique to the rest of the structure in that it was a circular tower that extended above the second story level of the rest of the manor. This piece of the architecture of the building would be the one in which Addie thought she might choose to place a library if she oversaw designing the layout. She gazed up at the topmost portion of the tower, which had a window facing in each of the directions that were visible to her, but if she were to bet money on it, she was sure that there were ones located on the others as well. When she focused and hit an angle where there was the least amount of glare, she could make out the shape of a good-sized telescope aimed towards the sky.

It only took her a short time to navigate the halls inside to find the entrance that led to the library. It was not necessary for Addie to guess at which one was the correct door, when she saw a metal plaque engraved with the image of an owl and the symbols spelling out the Goddess Athena's name in Greek. A room filled with books of collective knowledge would fittingly have the goddess of wisdom guarding it. She slowly pushed open the door, unsure if she should knock first, and peered in. Ruth had given her a little foresight that she might be in for a surprise, but it was exponentially better than she had expected.

Bookshelves lined every inch of wall space within the room. The space in the center was a circle of leather couches and chairs that looked so soft that they were practically inviting her to sink into one. In between each was a side table with a lamp to provide ample reading light no matter which spot you chose to sit in. Where the main portion of the room ended, as large as it was on its own, there were three steps up to another section. Addie crossed over to this area, noticing the floor as she made her way there.

Each square tile of flooring had strange textures to it and was lacking a definitive pattern from one to the next. Even the colors were mismatched amongst them, although they all had natural earth tones to them. Addie scooched down and ran her fingers across a particularly bumpy section of one of the tiles. It was difficult to make out what the long skinny object embedded into the tile was supposed to be, so she moved onto the next one. This tile was mostly a flat surface in a terracotta color, but in the corner, there was a tiny imprint which she had to get even closer to the floor to examine. "Oh, it's an ammonite." She smiled to herself, proud that she remembered what she had believed was an insignificant detail from her freshman year of biology class.

Moving on to the next one, she was able to pick out the bug-like shape of a trilobite more easily. As she progressed from one tile to the next, it became a game to find the object hidden in it and to try to guess what it was. Many of them contained just a small bone fragment which she knew were not human in origin. "Fossils. Each one contains a different fossil." Her passions in life had taken her on the path of human biology, and yet the other sciences fascinated her just as equally. The hidden relics within the floor could have kept her busy for hours, but the book still in her hand reminded her that there might be more treasures to be found in that room.

The three steps led to a circular room that was the base of the tower that Addie used as a guide to find the library. She stood in the center of it and looked up. Mirroring the main section of the room, there was not a single spot of wall space lacking a bookshelf. The only breaks in between were for the spiral staircase, which led to each level of the tower, and the little window nooks, allowing for cozy reading spots with natural light shining through. She followed the stairs up and around to each level, quickly perusing the selection of books along the way. There didn't appear to be a specific system used for sorting the collection, but the titles seemed to be ones from older texts the higher she rose.

At the very top of the tower, she tilted her head so far back that it became difficult to swallow. The dome of the ceiling was painted in a style resembling that of the works of Michelangelo. Below the artwork was a single window faced in each of the four directions with a tiny metal plaque attached to the frames, labeling them as north, south, east, and west. The telescope was as she had seen it from the outside, pointed up at the sky, but it would have been pointless to look in it without the view of the stars in the dark of night yet.

A small, intricately carved cabinet, with closed doors, and short wooden stool, were the only pieces of furniture in this level of the tower. What piqued Addie's interest was the basket filled with thin white gloves sitting on top of the cabinet. She lifted the hinge to release the latch and slowly swung open the door. A creak from the aged metal rubbing against itself echoed through the room. Addie cringed at the sound. As far as she knew, it was okay that she was in the library, but snooping through things hidden behind closed doors felt suspiciously wrong.

She felt her eyes widen at the sight of just a handful of titles displayed on individual stands within the case. The first one to grab her attention was a copy of *The Raven*. Not being a literature fiend, due to her scientific pursuits, it was the only book in the bunch in which she could recognize both the title and the author. Addie reached in to take a closer look at it, but just before her fingers touched the delicate binding, she pulled her hand away.

Armed with a thin white glove covering each of her hands this time, she protectively lifted the book from its stand. When she was sure that she had a good hold of the book with one palm fully supporting its weight, she used her other hand to open the front cover. Careful not to bend the binding too far back, she used her thumb to support the cover as if she were protecting the neck of a newborn baby. The title page did not offer information about which edition it was. There was only a date of eighteen forty-five, printed on the bottom of the page.

Addie read over the page a second time to grasp the meaning fully. "A first edition copy." As the words exited her mouth, she noticed that below the date where she thought a signature was printed in a different ink than the rest of the page. She could feel her jaw drop open. "A signed, first edition copy."

She stared back to the cabinet and the other books, which were given the same amount of care in their display space. Without taking the time to check each one, she was sure that they were either all first editions, signed copies, or as in the case with this one, both. Addie pondered over the idea that most museums would be fortunate to have even one of the treasures that was located in this building in their collection, let alone the many rarities she had stumbled upon in less than twenty-four hours of being within the manor walls.

"I never expected to find you in here." Gregory's voice boomed as it echoed up through to the dome of the tower.

The jolt of fear that shot through Addie's body at the sound of Gregory's approach almost shook the precious piece of history from her hands. "I'm just returning a book to the library." She could tell by the sound of his footsteps that he was close behind her.

"I'm quite astonished that you are well versed enough to read, or is that a picture book in your hands?"

"It's Poe, actually." Addie turned in order to better direct the return insult at him. "You should be familiar with his work. You seem to have the same stale humor as someone from the late eighteen-hundreds."

He did not seem to be concerned about her snide remark once he noticed the book in her hands. He did a nervous pace which only consisted of a few short, angry stomps before turning and doing it again, all the while, his hands were flapping uncontrollably. "Put that back immediately." He grasped onto the side of the cabinet door to help hold it open. "With the utmost of care, I might add."

She rolled her eyes as she followed through with his orders. Even though she would never admit it to him, she silently let out a sigh of relief at not having the responsibility of such an important object in her possession. "Maybe you shouldn't put out a fancy little basket filled with gloves, practically inviting people to touch the stuff in the case."

He glared at her. "If you are genuinely interested in this poetry, which I highly doubt you are, then you should pick up a recently printed copy in the downstairs portion of the library and keep your filthy hands off the Rosin families' private collection."

"I just might do that." Addie remembered what Ruth had told her about Nora having the final say regarding what anyone did. She tossed the gloves back in the basket and pulled out the book that she had jammed into the back pocket of her pants. "After I put back this book that I was asked to return to the library." She crossed her fingers behind her back in hopes that he would not ask who had assigned her the task.

"Hm, well, don't make a mess of the place." He plucked out the two gloves she had just worn with the tips of his fingers and held them away from his body as if they were disgusting and disappeared down the stairs.

Chapter Eleven

Addie waited until the sun had fallen below the horizon to make her exit. She could have gone at any time, since she was not being held against her will, but it only seemed fitting to complete her day and take her leave quietly and with the least amount of fuss possible. Earlier, she had inquired about the fence and learned that it did not actually extend around the entire perimeter of the property. It was meant to prevent unexpected visitors from driving up the driveway as well as to give the illusion of high security measures. Her plan was to bypass needing to have it opened for her, by way of exiting through the woods where the fence came to an end.

Dressed back in the outfit she had shown up in the day before, which had conveniently been washed and placed in her room, and her bag slung over one shoulder, she gingerly shut the door and made her way downstairs. The entryway was directly in front of her, but the chances of running into someone seemed higher than if she snuck out the rear exit. Even though the payoff for the rare violin, or the autographed first edition book, would be enough for her to be set for life, there was too much risk of getting caught for theft. They were both items that would be easily missed, so she opted to take only the large sapphire ring, which had been tossed into a drawer with so many others that one would have to search it out specifically before knowing that it was no longer there. The ring was currently hidden within the folds of her bag, so that if she were to have to go through a search of some sort, it would not be found or get accidently dumped out.

She navigated the halls with a stop and go motion, trying to be aware of any sounds of other people, while making her way as quickly as possible without looking too suspicious. All the while, in her head, she was disappointed in herself for lacking the courage to announce that she was leaving.

A twist of the doorknob later, she took a deep breath of relief that she successfully made it through the first hurdle of her journey. Even with the sky void of the sun, there was still plenty of light from the almost full moon, stars brighter out in the forested setting, and the multitude of solar lights scattered about the manor grounds. It was, however, the perfect amount of darkness to slip away in the shadows.

She crossed the lawn to an area of the property in which she had only been near previously that morning on horseback. A narrow path of flat stones, level with the grass surrounding it, led up to a great wall created by finely trimmed hedges. A white iron gate, purely for decorative purposes, served as the entrance to what Nora had described as her fairytale garden. Addie's plan was to follow along the outer edge of the massive structure, using it as cover, even though the chances of her being watched or followed were unlikely.

When she approached the gate, she noticed that it was slightly ajar. She was positive that when they went by earlier in the day, it was flush with the hedges. The only reason she remembered so clearly was because she was using anything to focus on to keep her mind off the fact that she was riding a horse. Using a single finger, she applied a little pressure to the gate, but it did not budge easily. The test showed that it could not have been merely the wind that blew it open.

She peered through the iron bars, trying to get a view of what lay on the other side of the thick bushes. Her eyes had already adjusted to the dim light, but something just beyond her line of sight still obstructed her view. Addie's goal was to get out of the gate surrounding Rosin Manor, and yet curiosity drew her to enter another one.

There was just enough space for her slip though without needing to open it any further, so she did just that. Only a few feet in front of her was a single tall hedge that created a barrier so that if anyone were to look through the gate, they could not see anything without stepping completely in. It was a unique way for a garden designer to create a privacy shield within the layout by keeping with the uniformity of the outer hedge walls.

Using the hedge as cover for herself, Addie crept to the edge, keeping her body behind it, and ducked her head around the corner. Thousands of tiny white lights illuminated the garden with a soft, sparkling glow. Typical of most gardens, there was an abundance of flowering plants, especially rose bushes, producing a pungent floral aroma in the air. What truly made the space a fairytale, as Nora had described it, were the many sculptures depicting fantasy creatures, dispersed in and around the meticulously manicured growth. Just from the spot she was standing in, she could see sculptures of a unicorn with a mane of ivy, a dragon breathing out a flame of red pansies, a phoenix surrounded in orange poppies, and countless little fairies dangling from the branches of trees. Addie had toured botanical gardens that paled in comparison to the floral diversity and works of three-dimensional art displayed here.

Little gusts of a summer breeze would periodically sweep through the garden, putting into motion every leaf and flower petal, sparking to life the stories hidden within the lavish display. Addie gasped as she looked down at her body that she had absentmindedly exposed as she had stepped away from the hedge while her surroundings mesmerized her. She was about to make her exit from the peaceful backyard paradise when she caught sight of movement at the far end of the garden.

The rustling of leaves had come to a standstill and yet she could still see motion from a figure. She crept a little farther into the garden, utilizing the shadows of some of the larger sculptures for cover. As she neared the center where a large fountain was the focal point for a water display, it was easier to get a view of the second half of the plot. From here, Addie could see the back of a granite bench, carved in the shape of an open book. On either side of it were iron hooks with lanterns hanging from them, illuminating the unmistakably long, shiny, black locks of Nora's hair.

From this vantage point, Addie could only see the back of Nora's head. It was just enough to keep her intrigued as to what she was doing out in the garden so late after sunset. With all the sparkling lights, it was no doubt a magical experience in the dark, but it still seemed like an odd place to enjoy the beauty of the flowers when their colors were less vibrant than in the daylight.

Addie glanced back at the exit. She could easily slip out without Nora knowing that she was ever there. Her perfect plan to escape without having to say goodbyes to any of the Rosin Manor dedicated lifetime members was within reach, and yet she couldn't peel her eyes away from the one resident that she regretted walking away from most of all. She silently cursed that she had convinced herself of the idea that she could have one last conversation with Nora before leaving for good.

She unslung her bag from her shoulder and tucked it just out of sight under the overhanging branches of a bush. Addie took each step in the white crushed rock pathway, bearing down her weight to make as much noise as possible during her approach. At the first sign of recognition, when Nora stirred in her seat, she announced her presence. "Don't be alarmed. It's just me."

Nora stood and flashed her an acknowledging wave. "Good evening, Addie." A gust of air swept up the light fabric of her white summer dress, so she tucked it back under her legs as she sat again.

Addie casually strolled to the bench and leaned over the back of it. "I hope I'm not interrupting you out here by yourself on this gorgeous summer night." She inconspicuously checked out the space in her lap to see if she was busy reading a book or maybe engrossed in her phone, as most people typically were.

In a gesture so slight and fast that it was almost missed, Nora scrunched her face and then raised her eyebrows added to a head tilt, to point to an area just in front of her. "Just paying my respects."

A few feet away, intermingled with a bed of

purple flowers, were two gravestones. Addie bowed her head down and placed her open hand on her own chest, over the space where her heart was located. "I'll leave so you can get back to that."

Nora's voice was so soft, it nearly got lost with the whistling of the wind. "Or you could join me and sit for a while."

Without hesitation, Addie rounded to the front of the bench and took the spot next to her. Each of the headstones were lit from below by small solar spotlights. The ghostly glow cast by the shine enhanced the depth of the shadows on the carved font of the matching Rosin name engraved on each of them. "Losing one parent is tragedy enough. I can't begin to imagine the devastation of both at the same time."

"Especially when I'm to blame for it."

"I remember when the plane crash that they were in made headline news. It was investigated thoroughly, and they concluded that it was an accident. How could you possibly believe that it was your fault?"

"It was an important business trip for my father, but my mother was planning on staying home, as she quite often did." Nora winced as if it was painful to even tell the story aloud. "I was invited to a party that weekend, so I convinced Dad to take Mom along with him for a vacation getaway. They took the family private plane, and as you know, it went down shortly after takeoff. My dad's partner and the pilot were also on board."

"It was a malfunction with the airplane. It was not your fault."

"Yes, my dad would have gone regardless, but for my own selfish reason, my mom is gone too."

Addie turned and held Nora's gaze. "There is no way you could have known what was going to happen. Do you feel like it is some sort of punishment to lock yourself up in the manor?"

"Possibly it was like that for the first few weeks, but eventually, everything changed."

"Changed how?"

Nora's brow furrowed as she gripped onto the edge of the bench. "It is difficult to explain, but after the sadness and feeling angry at myself all the time subsided, the fear started."

"Fear of leaving Rosin Manor?"

"Not just for myself, but I became consumed with the idea that if anyone left here, something might happen, and they would never come back again."

"That is when you made it so that no one would ever leave."

"I just could not bear the thought of losing another person."

Addie motioned to the area surrounding them. "This place may look magical, but it doesn't hold the power to protect people. Eventually everyone passes, even if it's from old age."

"I know that; I'm not living in some sort of fantasy world. I am well aware that eventually everyone dies. A year ago, the elderly woman who was my nanny since I was an infant died of cancer." Nora sighed heavily before moving on. "The difference was that I was by her side through all of it. Most importantly, I had the chance to say goodbye to her. She didn't just disappear from my life."

"Okay, I see the difference, but don't you think your parents would be devastated to know that you are living like this?"

"Tell me what is beyond these borders that is so important, that I'm missing out on?" Nora pointed aimlessly up in the air and then directed it to Addie. "I mean, what have you done with your life that makes it any better than mine?"

Addie released a long, frustrated breath, and pressed the palm of her hand to her forehead. "You got me there. I haven't accomplished much, and I've failed at a lot of things." She stood and rubbed at the back of her neck. "Although, I don't regret anything that I've learned from what I've done. Just ask yourself if you would ever look back on your life and regret never leaving Rosin Manor."

The haunted stare of Nora's eyes, lost in her own thoughts, was too heartbreaking for Addie to deal with. She took a few steps over to the crushed stone path, prepared to leave for good this time.

"Addie?" Nora's voice cracked as she softly called out her name.

Addie stopped in her tracks. "Yes?"

"I'm glad you came here." Nora paused. "To the manor, I mean."

She could feel her heart thumping in her chest. "Me too, Nora. I'm glad I came here too."

Addie strode out of the garden, scooping up her bag as she went. There was no stopping to enjoy the flowers on her way, and instead of slipping through the gate, she pushed through it, out into the open yard. A shiver coursed through her body, but she blamed it on the lack of a barrier against the wind.

She stood in one place, feeling lost, while she tried to process through the conversation that she just had with Nora. Just a short time ago, she had a plan and was on her way to execute it, before getting sidetracked in the garden. Addie looked in the direction of where she was headed to, but it seemed so dark and cold compared to the sparkling lights she had just walked away from. To her other side was the brightly lit manor, inviting and warm. Before she had fully convinced herself that it was the right decision to stay just a little while longer, she found herself walking up the grand staircase and down the hall.

As she approached her room, she paused with her hand on the doorknob, but made the last-minute decision to continue to the master bedroom. Once inside, she went straight to the closet where she slid open the drawer filled with rings. Addie stuffed two of her long fingers into the hidden fold of fabric in the bag and pulled out the shimmering translucent blue sapphire. She spun the ring a few times, admiring the clarity of the cut as it caught the light. With a gentle toss, she let it rejoin all the other precious stones. With a satisfied sigh, she turned and rummaged through the clothing on the opposite side.

On her way out, she flipped the switch to the closet lights, and gasped as she almost walked headfirst into Gregory. She pressed her hand against her chest. "It might be nice if you announced that you were coming up behind someone like that." She let out a nervous laugh.

"There should not be a need to announce myself in a room that you are not allowed to be snooping in."

"Well, remember how Nora gave me permission to wear what I wanted from the closet?" Addie raised her eyebrows and exaggerated her words slowly. "I kind of need to go through this room to get to it."

"If that is true, then what have you filled your bag up with?"

"Exactly what I said. Clothes to wear for tomorrow."

"What kind of a fool do you take me for?" Gregory shook his finger at her. "I distinctly heard the jewelry drawer open."

She tugged the bag down from her shoulder and held it out to him. "Go ahead and search it."

He raised his head up and looked at her offer with disgust, but just as quickly snatched the bag out of her hand. Gregory pulled out a shirt and a pair of pants, both with tags dangling from them. "These are quite impressive choices for working in."

She gestured to his current outfit. "You seem to get your work done fine in a suit. Everyone at Rosin Manor, even Lisa under her apron, dresses to the nines to do their jobs." She grabbed the wad of clothing from his hand and shook the wrinkles out. "This particular outfit though, is for the dinner and a concert date that Nora and I are attending together tomorrow evening. I'm sure she'd be disappointed if I went looking like this."

"I have been notified of this *function* of yours." Gregory glared at her then turned his attention back to the bag still in his hands. He shook it vigorously while peering in at a distance as if something might jump out at him. "As soon as I prove that you stole from Miss Rosin, there will be no dinner date for you."

"Search all you want, but there's only one item left in the bag." She stuck her hand in and pulled out a thick scrapbook. On the cover was her nickname scribbled out in messy handwriting with black marker and surrounded by a thick layer of stickers. There were sparkly colorful bits of rainbows and hearts sticking out from the bottom, but replaced by band stickers, equality symbols, and the one that is handed out on voting day, on top.

"What is hidden in that ghastly thing?"

"Oh, Gregory, I was hoping you would ask." Addie let the widest fake grin she could muster spread across her face. She tucked the folded clothes under one arm so that she had the use of both hands to properly display the book to him. She turned to the first page, holding it up as if she were reading an illustrated book to a young child. She tapped her finger on a black and white sonogram photo. "This is the very first photograph of myself." She slid her finger over to the next one, of an infant in a hospital bed next to a happy and tired looking woman. "This is the only picture I have of my mother and me together." She pointed to an obituary clipping from a newspaper. "Complications during childbirth are so much higher than one would think."

"Enough already." Gregory put his hand up to stop her from continuing.

She flipped the page anyway. "We are just at the beginning. I have so much more to tell you about." She showed off a blue ribbon taped to the thick cardstock page. "This was my first award in preschool."

"Just stop. I've heard too much about your pathetic life." He turned the bag upside down and tilted his head under it to get a better look. "Ah ha." A small flap hanging down caught his eye and he pulled open the pocket it was attached to. In rapid succession, three tampons dislodged from the pocket and bounced off Gregory's face on their way down to the floor.

"I'm not sure if that was more embarrassing for me or you, but by all means, continue looking if you must." She tried her best to hold in the snicker escaping from her.

He tossed the bag down to the floor. "Miss Rosin might be naïve enough to trust a total stranger around her family's jewels, but I still do not. I will do what I must in order to protect the lady of the house."

"For the record, I do not intend on hurting her, but go ahead and do whatever you think you need to do. I have a great idea." Addie pretended to be headed towards the door and flagged him to follow her. "We should find Nora and tell her that you need to strip search me for stolen items, but it will be your responsibility to explain why, if you don't find anything."

"Fine, you got away with whatever you were doing this time." Gregory let out an angry grunt. "I suggest you work on getting your own wardrobe soon. These clothes are not very flattering for a woman." He shot her an icy glare before stomping out of the room.

Chapter Twelve

Addie reached for the tray of food before Lisa had the opportunity to set it down on the counter. "I've got this."

Lisa wiped her hands off on her apron and gave Addie a stern look. "Last time, you came back with a full tray of food. Let's not have a repeat performance, lest Miss Rosin might wither away."

"Trust me, with the amount of butter and sugar you use in your cooking, we have nothing to worry about." Addie shot her a huge grin and swiftly crossed through the hall into the dining room.

Only once along the way, the momentum caught up with her and a splatter of juice spilled over the edge of the glass. She carefully set the tray down in front of Nora and lifted the lid.

"Does Lisa have you helping with kitchen duties?" Nora reached for the side dish of fresh fruit.

"No, I just wanted to redeem myself from last time. Well, that, and I also wanted to make sure everything was okay after last night's conversation. I hope I didn't overstep any boundaries by questioning your grieving process."

"I appreciate you seeing it as a process. It has been called worse by many people over the years."

Addie nodded her head. She pointed to the lid in her hand, proud that she had completed her task properly this time and started towards the door.

"Enjoy your breakfast."

"I do believe I promised you dinner before the show, so meet me at the stables at five o'clock tonight."

"Stables?" Addie stopped and turned back. "I thought my end of the bargain was taken care of already?" Despite the nauseated sensation at the thought of another horse ride, the jovial laugh coming from Nora warmed her insides.

"Don't worry, we are just going to have dinner somewhere special and we can't get there without transportation from something at the stables. I promise, it's not a horse."

"For the record, I'm not fond of other large animals either, so you better not expect me to ride on camels, elephants, or any other creatures you have hidden in that barn."

Nora grabbed a piece of toast from her plate, tore off a section of the crust and tossed it at Addie. "Don't be a smart ass or I'll make you ride a donkey to dinner."

Addie pointed to the chunk of bread that had bounced off her thigh and rolled onto the floor. "Hey, it better not be my job to clean up the mess you're making."

"Speaking of jobs, I have something for you to do today."

Addie ambled over to Nora's side and leaned against the table. "What would you like for me to do, Miss Rosin?"

Nora's face started to blush, and she was slow to get out what she was going to say, covering it up by clearing her throat. "As we speak, the room you stayed in the past two nights is being emptied out. A shipment should be arriving shortly. I took the liberty of ordering you some clothes, furniture, and other items you might need. These are just to get you by until you pick out exactly what you like. So, your project is to spend the day making that space yours."

"I thought I was getting a room in the same area as the rest of the staff?"

The sound of Nora's fork as she dropped it to her plate rung with a piercing ting. "Do you not like the room?"

"Of course I do." She eyed the fork, imagining Lisa's reaction if she returned after another failed attempt at delivering a meal. "That is, if you're okay with me invading the space in your wing of the house."

"If it wasn't okay with me, then you wouldn't be there in the first place." Nora waved her off. "Now go, before I change my mind."

⚛⚛⚛⚛

After tightening the last screw on the frame of her new bed, Addie lay underneath it and stared up at the ceiling through the openings between the slats. She had never built a piece of furniture, and the sense of accomplishment left a satisfying feeling in her. She slid the box spring and the mattress that were leaning against the wall onto the frame and tested the comfort of it with a bounce of her body. After years on a small dorm bed, followed by many more on an old broken mattress on the floor, this would be the best night's rest she would get in a long time.

"This should be the last of the boxes." Gregory stood in the doorway with a gloomy expression on his face. "I'm just going to place it over there with the others."

Addie sat up. "That's fine. Thanks for all your help. There was a lot more stuff than I was expecting." She glanced around the room at all the stacks of packages.

"I only did what Miss Rosin asked of me. Don't think that this was a gesture of kindness on my part."

"Don't worry, I wouldn't give you that sort of credit."

Gregory seemed to ignore her response, stepped farther into the room with his hands on his hips, and looked around. "I hope you're aware of just how much Mr. Rosin loved this room. He would sit by the window in the afternoon to read the paper and have tea."

"It was also where Mrs. Rosin practiced her music. There was a stand with sheet music on it."

He crinkled his nose and a smug look crossed his face. "Yes, well, either way, this was a sacred space with class to it." He waggled his fingers at the new modern furniture and decorations, all in shades of gray with subtle blue accents. "Now, you have desecrated it with all this junk."

"None of this was my idea. Take it up with Nora if you have a problem with it. I'm just as much a willing pawn in this situation as you are."

"I knew this was all a game to you. Miss Rosin will find out soon enough and when she does, I will be the first to see you out the door." Gregory shook his fist in the air. He took one last look in the room as if it were a destroyed monument, then awkwardly attempted to slam the too heavy door on his way out.

Alone in the room, Addie repeated the last words that Gregory spoke in a sarcastic tone and stuck her tongue out at the end, mocking his childish ways. The thought of his threats loomed over her, but if she didn't do anything wrong, he had nothing to hold against her. She decided not to let his empty words take away from the wonderful things Nora had provided her with and the excitement of what was to come later that day.

One box that stood out amongst the stacks scattered about the room was marked with bright red stickers, warning that it was fragile and should be handled with care. Addie sat cross legged on the floor and peeled open the cardboard box with the utmost care. Surrounded by a padding of recycled packing materials was yet another box. This one was unmarked by anything that would give away the identity of its contents.

She took her time, savoring every moment as if it were the last gift to open at the end of a birthday party. As she lifted the flap to the box, she let out an excited gasp. The unmistakable shape of a molded violin case made her shiver with joy. The last violin she had owned was the same instrument she learned on in middle school. It was one of the few beloved personal items that traveled with her to college and was a devastating loss to her when she had to sell it to make ends meet.

After raising the lid, applying the rosin to the tightened hairs of the bow, and tuning the strings, she played her first few notes on it. The sound projected out and came back to her as the vibrations resonated through her body. She could have played it for hours on end, but she forced herself to cut it short after one song. There was more work to be done, and an evening to prepare for.

When tuning the violin strings, she had purposefully denied her eyes from wandering anywhere near the interior of the sound hole. She did not want to persuade her ears to judge the quality of the sound based on who made the instrument. Her father had purchased her an intermediate model to learn on, which was a way better quality one than most school rentals. She chose never to upgrade since it sounded beautiful and she had no desire to pursue a career in music.

Having experienced this one, and pleasantly delighted by the tones, if only for a few moments, she was curious of its origins. She tilted the violin and read the label inside. "An Amedeo Simonazzi." She was shocked that she was even holding a piece created by such an infamous maker, but even more so that it was hers. It was no comparison to the one she played the other night, but it was impressive, and held a hefty price tag to show it. "This has to be a mistake."

Addie reached for the packaging and checked the mailing label. It clearly showed that the attention was to her personally. While she was grateful beyond words for the thoughtful gift, she lingered on the address.

The house she had been staying at previously could not be considered an official residence. She was not sure of the circumstances in which Mason had procured it, but she was not allowed to use the address associated with it on any of her documents. There were constant reminders that they might have to up and go at any time if their location was compromised to the wrong people. By *wrong*, Addie was told that meant authorities, clients, and any friends or family, all of which could never know where they resided. It was strictly a place to crash at night and earn a buck or two working for Mason's illegal business.

Seeing her name, even if it was only her first, attached to an address, was surreal. She swiped away the tears welling up in her eyes. Addie used a box cutter to remove the rectangle piece of cardboard containing the address. Using a piece of electrical tape from the toolbox she used to build her new bed, she stuck the new memory to a page in her scrapbook. There was a strong possibility that her time at Rosin Manor would be short lived, but it would always hold a place in her heart.

Chapter Thirteen

Addie approached the stables, wiping the sweat off the palms of her hands onto her hips as she walked. She could see Nora facing in the opposite direction, doing precisely the same motion as her, and it brought a smile to her face. As she neared, the sound of her footsteps hitting the gravel in front of the barn alerted Nora to her presence.

Nora turned while simultaneously checking her watch. "Right on time." Her eyes quickly darted the span of Addie's body. "You look good."

"I hope you like it. You did pick them out for me." She paused to show off the designer jeans and white, sleeveless blouse she was wearing.

"I thought it would be an interesting take on the clothes you came here in, but please feel free to order whatever you'd like if they aren't your style." Nora looked shyly down at the ground. "I will miss seeing you in those suit pants you had on yesterday though."

"Just say the word and I can make it happen again. That is, if the closet police don't stop me."

"Gregory?"

"How did you guess?"

"He's a little overprotective. I can have a talk with him, though."

"Overbearing is more like it, but don't bother. It's something that I need to work out with him."

"Okay, but please come to me if you need me to

intervene." Nora's face transitioned from a furrowed brow to the one that showed off the dimple on her cheek when she smiled. "Let's get going." She walked with a bounce to her step to the barn door and slid it open.

Parked behind the door was a four-wheeler with chrome polished so shiny, you could see yourself in it, and giant knobby tires that could traverse any terrain. Addie could feel her mouth drop open with excitement. "Now *this* is my kind of ride."

Nora straddled the wide seat, turned the key, and revved the engine. "Hop on."

Addie took her place on the remainder of the seat behind her. The way the seat was molded at an angle forced her to slide right up against Nora. It was a welcome feeling to be pressed up against the silky fabric of her all-black outfit that paired perfectly with her black hair. "You look stunning tonight."

"Thank you. I wouldn't consider it as elegant as you're making it seem, but it will do for the little surprise I have in store for you. I suggest you hold on for the ride."

Addie wrapped her arms loosely around Nora's waist and leaned in closer to her ear. "Don't worry. I won't let you fall off."

"Someone's a little confident when she's not on a horse." Nora shot a grin over her shoulder and hit the throttle. "By the way, it's me who will make sure you don't fall off."

The four-wheeler jerked as it took off fast out of the barn and across the lawn. Astonished by the speed that they were moving, Addie squeezed her arms a little tighter around her. She had to yell over the motor to be heard. "I'll admit, I wasn't expecting that."

Nora eased up slightly so that it wasn't so loud for a moment. "You'll probably say that again when you see where we're headed."

The engine whirred as it kicked into gear and they took off towards a trail into the woods. The first time they had entered here on horseback, Addie was too terrified to notice that there were multiple trails that ran off from one another. They randomly took turns here and there and it made her wonder if she could ever find her way back alone if she needed to.

Just as the maze of trees began to feel like an endless path, they pulled into a clearing in the woods. Within the open space, it looked as though a mix between a wedding, and a circus had set up camp there. A tall white gazebo formed the centerpiece. Surrounding it was a large white canvas tent and one other structure that a giant white sheet concealed. Every pole, stake, and tree trunk were wound with tiny white lights. They were also intertwined through each piece of lattice work on the gazebo and along the borders of the walkways leading to the tent and outer edge of the clearing.

Addie wondered how all of this could be possible so far into the woods, until Nora cut the engine to the four-wheeler and the low hum from a generator could be heard from behind the tent. While she was busy trying to get a view between the flaps of the canvas, Henry and Ruth slipped through one of the openings and approached them.

"Good evening, ladies." Ruth offered her hand to Addie.

It seemed silly to her to go through fake motions of being assisted when it was unnecessary. Addie looked to the opposite side of the ATV where Henry was helping Nora down. It occurred to her then that in Nora's circumstance, these minor instances of touch between herself and her staff might be the only source of human touch that she received. So, she, in turn, reluctantly accepted the offer from Ruth.

Nora came around to meet her and Addie was pleasantly surprised that she took her hand to guide her towards the gazebo. Three steps up brought them into a sturdy construction that looked to be newly built. There was a slight tackiness as she took a couple of steps across it, and a waft of fresh paint scent lingered in the air. The centerpiece of the gazebo was a table set for two.

The setting for their dinner this evening couldn't be any more perfect. It was unique, cozy, and intimate. The only negative part that Addie wished she could change was Gregory's presence, standing behind the table with a smug look on his face. He pulled out a chair and bowed his head to Nora. When she was seated, he took the napkin, which was folded in the shape of a swan, gave it a quick whip, and guided it gently to her lap.

Addie would have been content with seating herself, but she caught Nora giving the direction to Gregory to give her the same treatment. He looked like he'd rather pluck out his own hair one strand at a time, so she waited patiently while he cycled through the uncomfortable steps that he just did for Nora. While it was amusing for her to watch him squirm at having to serve someone who should be taking direction from him, she was glad when he finally finished and scuttled off to the tent.

She sighed contentedly and took another look

around the picturesque gazebo. "This place is like an amazing hidden oasis. It appears to be built just recently, and by recent, I mean today."

"I wanted to feel like I was somewhere new and different for our dinner tonight, so I had it made for us today."

"You created all of this in one day?"

"It's amazing what you can accomplish with unlimited funds."

"Speaking of funds, the violin was a very generous gift."

"It was nice hearing music coming from that room again." Nora spun the glass of ice water on the table. Beads of condensation dripped down the sides and pooled on the coaster it was sitting on. "After I heard the way you played the Stradivarius, I felt like you should have something of a higher quality than a standard instrument."

"Well, thank you, and I promise to play for you often, in return."

Nora reached her hand across the table and ran her finger across the top of Addie's hand. The contact was so light that Addie could hardly feel the pressure of it, and yet it caused a tingling sensation across every inch of her body. Just as she was about to flip her hand over to return the touch, Nora quickly pulled her hand away.

Fearing that she had overstepped a boundary, Addie searched Nora's face for a reason. All she found though, was a stoic, picturesque look staring off into the distance. Addie started to shift nervously in her chair, until the answer literally came up from behind her. All in a row, Henry, Ruth, and Gregory came up with plates of salad, bowls of soup, and beverage options filling their hands. They marched through like little soldiers, dropped off the meticulously plated food, and disappeared back through the tent flap just as fast as they had come.

"Sorry about that." Between the hum of the generator, the thick canvas walls of the tent, and the forested atmosphere surrounding them, there was little chance of anyone overhearing, but Nora leaned over the table and spoke softly. "When the people who work for me are also my closest friends, or more like family, it makes me feel like it's difficult to get to know you physically without the prying eyes of everyone else." She tapped the top of Addie's hand, toying with the possibility of holding it again.

"I completely understand." A wave of relief at not being the cause for Nora's rejection rippled through her, yet the feeling was short lived.

Addie's throat felt suddenly dry and constricted. She reached for the glass of iced water and took a gulp. Up until this point, she had made decisions based on her own needs. She admitted to herself that she changed her mind a couple of times due to how things might affect Nora. Yet, those changes were because it was ultimately what she chose to do. With the shift in Nora's view of her, as an interest beyond friendship, her ability to up and leave on a whim had now become complicated.

She took another gulp of water and glanced at Nora to deduce whether she may have caught on to the withering mess that Addie had turned into. Nora's face displayed a dignified smile, but along with it, Addie caught a glimpse of nervous excitement as she worked at pouring two glasses of wine for them.

Nora set a glass in front of Addie and raised the

other one up. "A toast to dinner away from the manor dining room."

She followed suit and raised her glass. "Cheers to that, and to our night out at the show afterwards."

Their glasses met above the center of the table with a clink. Addie took a tiny sip, not caring much for the bitter taste of the red wine, but also anxious about the doubtful look that Nora gave in response to her toast.

Nora darted her eyes away from her and busied herself with choosing the correct fork for her salad. Before using it to eat, she waved it up in the air like a wand. "How about some music with our dinner?"

Right on cue, Ruth lowered and whisked away the white sheet covering the mystery structure. Revealed was a stage just large enough to fit two women with guitars, microphones, and speakers. Without introduction, the lead and rhythm guitars started up into a familiar tune. When the vocals began and the harmony joined in for one of their popular hits, any previous feelings of unease were lost to Addie in the excitement of the moment.

"Are you serious? You got the Woo Girls to play for us here before their show tonight?"

Nora winked from across the table. "I have my ways."

Over the course of a setlist of songs in the background, they enjoyed a barbeque dinner, which paired perfectly with the atmosphere of the forest. The timing was perfect when the last bite of strawberry cheesecake was scooped up on her spoon and the music petered out with the last few strums. Not only did she and Nora give them a standing ovation, but everyone else who had emerged from the tent after dessert was served to have a picnic dinner and enjoy the end of the show.

The two musicians set their guitars down in the readily open cases, bowed, and waved to the small audience. One of them approached the microphone again while the other hurried to gather their gear. "It was an honor playing for you, but we have to rush out of here to make it to our next gig on time."

From behind the stage area, a large all-terrain vehicle pulled out, towing a trailer behind it. The limo driver from the first day Addie had come to Rosin Manor hopped out and made quick time of loading up their equipment and whisking them away down the trail.

Addie washed down the last bite of the sweet ending to their dinner with a sip of water and removed the napkin from her lap. "We should get going too if we want to catch the beginning of their show."

Nora's face contorted into a furrowed brow and she sucked her bottom lip in, before letting it pop back out. "We just saw them perform."

She heard the words that Nora spoke, and yet the rustling of movement as everyone disappeared beneath the tent distracted her. The little clearing, which moments before was bustling with music and activity, was now cloaked in an eerie silence. Addie refocused herself back to the subject at hand. "Yes, and the private concert was lots of fun, but the deal was to *go* to their show."

"True, I specifically repeated *go* back to you, but in the agreement, it wasn't defined exactly where we were going to. Technically, this location counts."

"You have got to be kidding me." Addie shook her head. She wasn't sure if she was more disgusted by the fact that Nora had just taken advantage of her, or at herself for falling for it. "I can't believe you."

"Oh, come on. I thought you had fun tonight."

"That's not the point and you know it."

"I don't understand what the problem is. We both got what we wanted and had fun doing it. Why are you so upset?"

"The whole point of the deal was to help overcome our fears."

"Easy for you to say. All you had to do was ride on the back of a horse."

Making her situation seem insignificant with a single statement that stung as if she had just been slapped caused a heat of anger to rise in Addie. The only thing that calmed it was that she hadn't shared the story behind her fear. "When I was a kid, my stepmother forced me into riding lessons to keep me out of her hair. One day, my horse got spooked, bucked, and threw me against a tree trunk." She sucked in a breath, reliving the whole experience through her story. "I broke rib bones, my leg, and arm. Horses scare me more than anything. So, if you weren't serious about going to the show with me tonight, then you should have just said no. I would have understood."

Addie could see the regret in Nora's downturned lips, but nothing about the romantic atmosphere of the little forest paradise could compel her to stay and face the person who disappointed her so harshly. She pushed her chair back, bounded down the gazebo steps, and within seconds, was on the trail surrounded by nothing but trees.

Zero thought was put into the plan for navigating the trail system back to the manor before she took off in haste. For the time being, though, it was a straight path, and the tire marks from the trailer that recently passed through left visible ruts along the trail floor for her to follow.

As she ventured farther away from the clearing, she found herself swatting at the buzz of mosquitos attacking her exposed skin. With all the excitement of the band and distraction of delicious food, she hadn't paid much attention to the lack of insects that typically accompanied outdoor events. She pictured herself back in the gazebo and it came to her that the air smelled less of the woody scent as it did now and was instead heavy with a citrus aroma. "Citronella candles." The sound of her own voice spoken aloud, alone in the forest, brought goose bumps to the surface of her skin. She slapped away another bite to her elbow and quickened her pace.

Chapter Fourteen

It was difficult for Addie to judge how long she had been walking, but it couldn't have been any more than fifteen minutes if she had to guess. To ward off the ongoing battle with the bloodsucking bugs, she shoved her arms down into her shirt to give them less access. This in turn, though, made for a less balanced walk on the rough terrain, and she stumbled unsteadily over rocks and tree roots.

A part of her wanted to admit that it was unwise to take off alone on foot, in pursuit of expressing her disapproval of Nora's deceitful attempt to satisfy a bet. The other part of her stubbornly trudged on despite the unpleasant travel conditions.

The idea crossed her mind on a couple of occasions to shave off some distance by cutting directly through the forest in the general direction of where she believed the manor to be located. In one area, where the trees appeared to be less dense than others, she entered a few paces in, only to be met in the face by sticky strands of a spider web. She promptly turned back, and spent the next few minutes frantically checking her body over for unwanted creatures.

Every little sound that the woods offered caused panicked jumps from Addie until she caught sight of the source. Most often it was birds taking flight up to the sky from the treetops, chipmunks dropping acorns from their perches, or mice darting across her path. It wasn't until the familiar sound of an engine approaching in the distance behind her that she let out a relaxed breath. She popped her arms out from her shirt, straightened out her shoulders, and swung her arms to set a determined pace.

Without looking behind, she moved aside on the trail to make room for whoever it was to pass. She decided that if it were anyone other than Nora, that she would gladly accept the offer for a ride back if it was made to her. With the sheer number of people and supplies that needed to pass through on their way out, she was sure to get some reprieve from this horrendous hiking experience.

The four-wheeler pulled up beside her and crawled along at her pace. Without stopping to acknowledge the driver, Addie caught sight of the flash of black hair and continued moving forward as if everything was fine.

Nora revved the engine and passed her but came to a stop not far ahead. "I don't expect you to accept this as an excuse, but I've had almost no social interaction with anyone other than the staff here in over seven years. They have basically become accustomed to how I go about dealing with things."

Just as she reached the spot where Nora had stopped, Addie slowed to shoot her a glare. "Sorry I didn't *comply* with your staff code of kissing your ass no matter what you do." She continued walking past.

The engine roared back to life and once again, Nora pulled up just ahead of her and stopped. "The others accept what I do because they are like family; they're not here for anything materialistic that I can offer them."

"If it was material things that I was after, then

I would have taken the fifty-thousand-dollar violin you gave me and left. Instead, I'm in the middle of the forest getting eaten alive by bugs, after being scammed by someone I thought I could trust." Addie kept her pace up as she approached Nora, without the intention of stopping.

"What I did was wrong. I let my fear take over and fell back into the old habit of using my resources to get out of having to face my problems."

Addie stepped around the four-wheeler. "There are some things that money can't buy."

"Wait, please. Let me make this up to you."

Addie slowed. "Going to the show at this point doesn't seem like a good idea." She turned back to see that Nora was already creeping up steadily behind her.

"I agree. I'm not in any way prepared to do something like that." Nora reached out and grazed her hand down the back of Addie's arm. "I do owe you an experience, though, that equally tests my fears. Will you please come with me?"

For a long moment, Addie made it appear as though she was putting a great deal of thought into the decision. In the meantime, her body twitched about with the idea of how many welts from bites were scattered about her skin. "Can I drive?"

A smirk spread across Nora's face as she slid back on the seat. "Go for it."

It felt exhilarating to be in control of the powerful vehicle that gripped the rough trail floor and tore across the terrain as if it were gliding atop it. Even better was the feeling of Nora's arms wrapped around her waist, and the press of her chest against her back. The best sensation, though, was at path intersections, when Nora's hand slid down the thigh matching the direction in which she needed to turn.

Once they reached the opening that led to the backyard, Addie eased into the throttle with her thumb until they were steadily crossing the lawn at top speed for the motor. As they neared the barn, she slowed to a smooth stop.

Nora made no attempt to let go of her one-sided embrace. "Take us up to the manor gate, please."

Without question, Addie took her foot off the brake and continued in a wide arch around the manor. She welcomed the extra time to have the closeness of Nora paired with the freedom of the air blowing in her hair as they sped up the driveway.

Addie leaned against the gate, while she watched Nora fiddling with the keypad. She pretended to be interested in scratching at one of the insect inflicted wounds to her wrist, while committing to memory the numerical code that opened the gate. She stepped aside as the metal bars slid apart and separated to leave an opening the same width as the driveway. "Do you mind me asking what it is we're doing out here?"

"I haven't been beyond this point in over seven years. This is one of my greatest fears, and I'd like to face it, if you're willing to accept, as my end of the bargain."

"Thank you for recognizing the inadequate way you handled our deal, and yes, I accept your offer."

Nora flashed a nervous smile. "Please remain where you are. This is something I have to attempt on my own."

Addie nodded her head and planted her feet into a mound of dirt and grass. She folded her arms and settled in against the iron bars of the gate. "I'll be here if you need me."

She watched as Nora followed along the outside of the gate for approximately fifty feet and then hopped lithely over the ditch to the edge of the pavement. The road was not a heavily traveled one, but Nora triple checked in both directions before crossing it as if it were a highway during rush hour traffic. After safely stepping off the pavement to the gravel on the opposite side, she continued a little farther down the road. Firmly standing guard at her post, it became increasingly more difficult for Addie to see the details of what Nora was doing as she wandered away. It was a bit of a relief when she finally came to a stop and bent to reach for something in the tall grass. When Nora turned, the glowing smile at having picked a handful of wildflowers brought a matching one to Addie's face.

She stood her ground as instructed and observed the calculated movements Nora made on her way slowly back. The way she scampered from one spot to the next reminded Addie of a nervous chipmunk, frightened of every little thing in its environment. Periodically, Nora would make eye contact with her, and Addie would offer an encouraging raise of her eyebrows to show her support.

With all the positive progress of the first outing, Addie began to envision the possibilities of what could come of this. She planned out the next few days and how they could venture out a little farther each time. By the time her deadline would be upon her, she just might have the ability to leave and be welcomed back when her debt was paid. So many ideas crossed her mind that she didn't hear the approach of the airplane overhead until she saw the flowers drop from Nora's hands.

The small airplane swooped low and glided above the tree line. Nora's motions were erratic as she started to rush back to the gate entrance. Her arms flailed about as if she were reaching for something, although there was nothing but the open road ahead of her. Upon her chaotic approach, she didn't put any attention into looking for potential vehicles that might be passing by. Not only was she in a precarious spot, but she didn't appear to be progressing forward.

Concerned for her safety, Addie darted across the road to meet her, but when Nora noticed, she was met with a look of pure terror. Addie saw arms and hands intersecting each other rapidly to get her to turn back. She was so close, though, that she chose not to heed the visual directions aimed at her.

At an arm's-length away, Addie reached out and pulled Nora into her embrace, while simultaneously turning to be on guard of oncoming cars in the lane they were standing in. When she was sure they were clear to cross, Addie attempted to usher her towards the gate entrance. She could feel Nora's body heaving for gasps of air as she fought through the panic attack. Addie assumed if she could only get her back on Rosin Manor grounds, that Nora would be able to calm down from her rattled state.

Unexpectedly, Addie felt Nora reverse the role and take the lead in guiding her. Nora's hand gripped onto the back of her shirt and practically pushed her along. When they were safely in the driveway, Addie was given a stiff little shove even farther away from the gate.

Nora's fingers practically pounded down on the buttons of the keypad, then she glared at the gate as if displeased at the lack of speed in which it was closing.

After it was securely shut, she extended her arms out and made the motion of squeezing the air in front of herself in frustration. "I asked you to stay where you were."

"I did, until you put yourself in a dangerous situation. You were practically frozen in the middle of the road."

"I was just stunned to see you defying something that you agreed to."

Addie opened her mouth to blurt out that she wasn't about to stand by and potentially watch her get hurt. As she did, the events of the last few minutes flashed in her mind. "Oh, it all makes sense now. You're less afraid for yourself than you are for me being outside the gate."

The panicked expression on Nora's face dropped to a blank stare. She motioned to the four-wheeler. "The keys are in the ignition. Please take it back to the barn for me."

"You don't have to avoid the subject with me. It's understandable that you would believe that keeping the people you care about behind these walls will keep them safe."

Nora's eyes welled up with tears. "Just return the four-wheeler to the barn, please." She turned and hurried down the driveway toward the manor.

As much as Addie yearned to chase after her, she knew that it was in her best interest to do as instructed. She took the long way back by taking a wide loop around the far side of the manor and then crossing the back lawn in a zigzag pattern before parking it just inside the barn doors. By this time, there were loads of supplies from the dinner setup being hauled out from the woods, and Gregory made sure to recruit her to help unload everything back to the kitchen as well as other respective locations.

When darkness set in, Addie retreated to the washroom to soak the aches from the tumultuous day away in a steamy bath. Afterwards, she found solace in playing through a list of classical songs on her violin. It filled her with pride that she could slowly stumble through most of them by memory alone. She cycled through the songs a second time, but this go around, she sped up the tempo and played vigorously.

Halfway through the set, she noticed a shadow move in the gap under her door. It remained there until she lowered her bow from the strings. As fast as she tried to reach the door and open it, the hallway was void of anyone in either direction.

Addie returned to her room and ran her fingers down the flamed maple back of her violin before nestling it into its case. She scanned the room to find a spot to store it, but out of habit of keeping her special possessions close, she set it on the bed next to her, and fell asleep with it at her side.

Chapter Fifteen

Addie sat up in bed and stretched, feeling refreshed after having slept on a quality mattress for the first time in years. She pulled the tags off some of the items in her newly acquired clothing collection, slipped into a jeans and tee shirt combination, and headed to the kitchen.

The tray of food was on the counter still, but everyone was seated around the table already. Addie lifted the cover and peered beneath it to find that it was untouched. "You folks weren't waiting for me to bring this in, were you?" She glanced up at the clock above the china cupboard to confirm that it was later than usual for Nora to get her breakfast.

Lisa projected her voice over her shoulder while expertly drizzling a swirl of frosting on her cinnamon bun. "She never came to the dining room this morning."

"Maybe I ought to check her room. What if she isn't feeling well?"

The maid, Francine, raised her hand to signal that she had something to say, but exaggerated the motion of finishing chewing her food first. "I went in to make her bed this morning, but it hadn't been slept in last night."

Going around the circle of people sitting at the table, Addie watched with confusion as they joyously went about eating their breakfast. "Why isn't anyone concerned about this?"

Lisa pulled the napkin from her lap and wiped her hands clean as she made her way over to Addie. She placed one hand on her shoulder when she got close enough. "Once you get to know Miss Rosin, you will learn how she deals with certain situations." She removed her hand and gave Addie a playful nudge with her elbow. "Trust me, a night not spent in her room and a missed meal are common occurrences."

"If you know her so well, then you know where I can find her."

"Hmm, I'm going to assume that you ladies did not part ways on good terms last night." Lisa flashed her a wink. "So, which was it that she was feeling, angry or sad?"

"I would have to say that it was a mixture of both."

"Ah, that's not good, for you anyway, but it's an easy answer for me. You'll find her on the fencing strip in the gym."

"The gym?"

After receiving detailed directions on how to get there, Addie made her way down to the basement. As she passed by multiple doors, she was amazed at just how many more rooms made up the lower level of the manor that she had never known existed.

The entrance to the gym was appropriately marked with the symbol of the Olympic rings carved and painted into the door. It opened to one large room sectioned off into different workout zones. She wandered past the cardio, boxing, and weightlifting sections, admiring the cohesive Olympic theme throughout the entire space. Mounted on the walls were some modern relics such as torches, jerseys, and even a set of metals. The interesting ones, though, were paintings, photographs, and artifacts, depicting the first games that took place in Athens, Greece.

In the far corner of the room, Addie could see the fencing strip. Sure enough, just as Lisa had suggested, Nora was in the center of the specialty aluminum sports flooring. She was lying directly across the center line, fully dressed in her protective gear. She was face up, staring at the ceiling, with her mask removed and resting on her stomach and fingers clasped around the foil to her side.

Thinking that it would be awkward to have a conversation standing above her, Addie started to crouch down, but ended up just joining her completely, in the opposite direction on the floor. She hooked a finger around the button tip of the foil and gave it a gentle shake, just enough so that Nora would be able to feel the vibration of the movement through the object in her hand. "I'm sure swinging this thing around in the air all night was not satisfying for letting out your frustration. So, how about if I give you a real target to hit?"

There wasn't a verbal response, but Nora pointed to a wall.

A series of hooks and shelves contained a wide array of options for fencing equipment. Addie hopped up and got suited up in her protective gear. The last part she reached for was the body cord which attached to the weapon to aid in electronic scoring.

"Don't bother with that. We can have a civil bout."

She hung the cord back on its hook. "If you prefer."

Addie met Nora at their respective lines on the strip. Without further discussion, they simultaneously raised their swords to a vertical position and then lowered them again in a salute.

Nora's lip curled up in a smirk. "En garde." She expertly placed her mask on her face with one hand and took a stance behind her line as she waited for Addie to follow suit. "Fence."

In a flurry of movement, Addie could see the tip of Nora's foil thrusting towards her. She parried the attack and lunged forward. Sure that a touch had been made, she lowered her guard, waiting for Nora to call the halt.

For a split second, Nora paused, but it was difficult for Addie to see her expression through the grates of the mask. The halt never occurred as Nora came at her in full attack mode. Acting swiftly, she was able to deflect the oncoming barrage of thrusts aimed at her. Using a combination of fast footwork and blocks, she was able to avoid any touches.

As they moved back and forth in an exchange of attack versus counterattack, Addie found herself feeling as though they were in a dance of sorts. There was a beauty in the flow of their movements. She was enjoying the feeling so much that she avoided scoring on Nora just to continue it longer. It became evident after a short span of time, by Nora's haphazard jabs, that she did not share in the mood. Addie decided it would be best to give them both a needed rest, so she went for a flashy move by whipping her blade in a flicking motion so that it curved and tapped Nora on the shoulder.

Proud of her accomplishment, and sure that Nora could not have missed the touch, she dropped her foil to her side and removed her mask. "That was a great bout." She tucked her mask under her arm so that she could offer her hand out to shake.

Nora tore her mask off and shook loose her long strands of hair that got stuck in the straps. She sneered at the offer to congratulate on the outcome of the game. "Who the hell are you?"

"Whoa, why are you asking that?"

Nora's face squeezed up like she tasted something bitter. "Oh, playing like you don't know."

"I really don't know what that's supposed to mean." Addie set down her mask and foil and made a calming motion with her hands, attempting to bring down the heightened level of anger that Nora was exuding.

"You're pretending to be some down and out girl from the city with a shady past looking for work."

"I'm not pretending."

"Do you take me for a fool who's too ignorant to see that you took riding lessons, you know the exact value of an Italian violin, and you know how to fence?"

"How is my being well-rounded and knowledgeable a problem?"

"You know damn well that only wealthy children are raised with all of that. So, I'm going to ask you again, who are you, and what are you doing here?"

"Look, in all honesty, you're right. I did have a similar childhood to yours. The difference is that as an adult, I've had everything taken away from me."

"How could you possibly lose everything?"

"I was just completing my third year of medical school when my dad passed. I was an adult and due to his lack of a will, my father's estate went to his wife of twenty years. I had no money to fight it, too much debt owed to Harvard, and no one willing to co-sign loans for my following years at school."

Nora's stiffly guarded stance shifted as her arms

dropped and her head tilted slightly to one side. "Losing a parent is difficult enough. I can't imagine how it must have been to suddenly be on the streets afterwards. I'm sorry."

"Enough years have passed for me to process and come to terms with it. I came here to get away from the downward spiral that I got sucked into. Are you willing to accept that I just want to forget about my past and please stop questioning me about it?"

A long pause passed and then Nora reached her hand across the space between them. Her fingers aimed down towards the floor. "I will respect your wishes."

Addie took her hand in acceptance and inched slowly closer to her. She held her gaze, staring intently into the magnificent hues of her brown eyes. She arched her head down so near that Addie could feel Nora's breath breaking against the wall of her chin. "How about we go another round?"

Nora playfully batted her away. "No way."

"Because you know I'll win again."

"I lost because I didn't get any sleep last night, and I'm starving. Let's go get something to eat."

"Touché."

Even though Nora assured her that it was acceptable to leave their equipment on the strip, Addie insisted on staying behind for a few extra minutes to organize everything back to its place.

In the kitchen, a very frantic Lisa rushed between the stove and the counter, cooking and prepping at the same time. "The meal isn't quite ready yet, but we can get her started by bringing the orange juice in."

"I'm on top of it." Addie carefully lifted the glass, thick with juicy chunks of pulp floating in it, and garnished with curled sliced orange twists along the rim. She moved across the hall and into the dining room with more speed than when trying to balance it on top of a tray.

Nora looked up at her from her seat when she entered the room. "That was fast."

"Don't get too excited. I only have a beverage, but Lisa will probably have the rest done by the time I get back in there." She set the glass down then turned to leave, but she only took a few steps when she felt Nora's hand wrapped around her wrist.

"I'd like for you to stay."

"While you eat?"

"Yes. Will you have breakfast with me?"

"I'd be honored."

Nora looked at the table and approached the chair adjacent to hers at the very end. She pulled it out and nodded to Addie. "For you."

"Shouldn't I be the one pulling out the chair for you?"

"Consider yourself off the clock for the time being."

"I was under the impression I was always on."

Nora nodded her head as if considering the idea. "Have the others been keeping you too busy with tasks?"

"Nothing I can't handle, as long as Ruth is just joking about the barn manure duty she keeps trying to recruit me for."

"Ha, she's always bragging about how it keeps her biceps in shape to shovel out the stalls. I doubt she'd give up that job."

The door swung open and Gregory walked in with the tray in his hand. "I'm not sure where Addie is, but isn't this her job?" He got a little closer and gasped when he noticed her sitting at the table.

Nora's eyes narrowed at his comment. "Return to the kitchen and have Lisa make a serving for Addie also, please."

He motioned to the chairs at the opposite end of the room. "Shall I have someone make up a place setting at the guest section of the table?"

Nora crossed her arms. "No, Gregory. She is fine where she is, thank you."

"With all due respect, that is Mr. Rosin's seat."

Nora shot up out of her own seat and got right up in Gregory's space. "I am aware of that, but you have no right to question my decisions. You know damn well that if my father were here, you would have no problem taking over my mother's seat." She pointed to the empty chair across from her own.

He stood, glaring daggers down at Nora for a moment. "Fine, I will return with her food."

"Don't bother. I've lost my appetite."

"Yes, Miss Rosin." Gregory spun on his heel and left abruptly.

Nora slid the tray of food in front of Addie. "I'm sorry for that. Please enjoy my meal so that Lisa's hard work doesn't go to waste." She turned towards the door.

Addie slid her arm across the front of Nora's waist and clasped her hand around her hip to prevent her from moving forward. "Wait. You've got to stop running every time things get difficult."

"I need you to understand that this is what I have to do right now."

Addie reluctantly dropped her arm and let her go.

Chapter Sixteen

The afternoon sun was sweltering, but Addie had found reprieve from it on a bale of hay in the shadow cast from the barn. It wasn't an ideal spot with the unpleasant scent of manure wafting out of the doorway, combined with the occasional whinny let out that made her jump out of her own skin.

The only reason why she chose this location was because there was a perfect view of Nora across the lawn. She was set up on a quilt in the center of the yard, protected from the sun's rays under a large parasol. Addie found it amusing that Nora seemed to be engrossed in a newspaper. It was something so rarely done by someone their generation other than a random digital article read on social media.

Ruth leaned her arms up on the edge of the haystack. "How's the book?"

Addie quickly diverted her attention off Nora and turned the page of the book she had in her hands. "Eh, it's okay."

Ruth plucked the book from Addie's hands, turned it from its upside-down position, and handed it back right side up. "Why don't you just go over there and talk to her?"

"It seems like a lot of our conversations end in her leaving. I've dealt with a lot of the same losses as her, but she won't let me in past the wall she's built up."

"My suspicion is that it is less about her parents and more about another loss which she suffered."

"Another?"

"I'm sure by now that you've heard about the party."

"The one that Nora wanted to go, which caused her to convince her mother to go on the trip too?"

"Yup." Ruth kicked a clump of caked on mud off her boot. "It was actually her girlfriend. They had been together for a few months before the accident."

"What about after?"

"She came to visit Nora often the first week. An eighteen-year-old only has so much patience dealing with someone else's grief, so she gradually stopped coming. When she didn't attend the funeral, Nora was devastated. Not only were her parents gone, but she lost her first love."

"That's why she won't open up to me. She assumes that I'll leave eventually too."

"I'm guessing that's the reason. Keep trying, though." Ruth nudged the side of Addie's sneaker. "I know you can get through to her somehow."

"What makes you so sure?"

"Because every time you're not looking up at her, she's looking over here at you."

Addie could feel the heat of the blush taking over her face. She turned away from Ruth and hopped down from the hay bale. "I better get on that then."

"Good luck."

Gathering the few supplies necessary didn't take Addie long, but the walk to, from, and through the manor did. As she approached the parasol she knew Nora was sitting behind, she slowed to compose her breath so that it didn't seem like she was winded. To avoid rejection, she chose to take a seat along the far edge of the quilt without asking for permission first. She set down the antique wooden metronome between them and on either side of it she laid out a silk tie.

Nora lowered the newspaper to her lap. "Those are some interesting items."

"They're for a game."

"A game using a metronome and ties?"

"Yup."

"Are you going to explain?"

"I'll tell you the rules as we're playing the game." Addie scooped up the items, stood, and offered her hand to Nora.

"I couldn't possibly pass on something that sounds so intriguing." Nora placed her hand in Addie's.

Their hands remained clasped together as Addie led her to the boundary of the lawn where it met with the woods. She took the two ties and hung them around Nora's neck. "Choose a tree somewhere out there. Any tree you want."

Nora scanned the area and pointed to a tree about forty yards into the forested area. "The one that stands above all the others with the branch that curves up at the top."

To be sure she got the right one in her sights, Addie stood behind her and followed the line made by her finger. "Got it. Wait here. I'll be right back."

Bounding out into the woods, Addie followed the straight line to the tree as well as she could, making quick work around obstacles such as branches, trees, and thick undergrowth. When she reached the thick trunk of the chosen tree, she wiped away the pile of debris at its roots. Smoothing out a flat surface in the soil, she set the metronome down and pulled the metal pendulum rod to one side to set it in motion. Satisfied that it was running steadily, she returned to where Nora was waiting.

"Did you just leave the metronome out there?"

"Yes, it's set, so now all we have to do is put on the blindfolds."

"Blindfolds? For both of us?"

"Uh huh." She winked as she rounded to position herself behind Nora and pulled up one of the ties from around her neck so that it covered her eyes. "Do you trust me?"

Nora's head bobbed slightly up and down. "Yes."

She pulled the red silk fabric so that it was secure around Nora's head, careful not to pull any of her shiny black strands of hair in the process. "Is that too tight?"

"No."

"Stay right there. I'm going to put mine on now." Addie removed the other tie from around Nora's neck. She was more careless putting her own on, just knotting it up and not caring how crooked or messed up her hair was underneath it. "Okay, I can't see anything. Can you?"

"Absolutely nothing."

"Good, now just reach out for me." Addie stretched out her arms in Nora's direction and waited until she felt her fingertips brush her own. She wrapped her hand around Nora's wrist and guided their bodies closer together. "The goal of the game is to try and reach the tree you picked out."

"It sounds a little scary with both of us unable to see."

"I won't let anything happen to you. I promise. Do you trust me enough to give it a try?"

"I do."

"Good, let's get started. So, from here, do you remember where the tree was located?"

"Straight in front of us." Nora's voice was low and timid sounding.

"Okay, so stretch your arm out in front of you. Keep swinging it slowly from side to side. That will protect the upper half of your body. When you step, point your toe out and test your step before you take it. That will protect the lower half." She gripped her arm firmly around Nora's waist. "Most importantly, don't leave my side."

Nora pressed her body in even closer to hers. "Got it."

Taking the lead, Addie proceeded forward slowly, guiding Nora to advance with her. The first couple of steps were awkward as they learned to move together as one, but in the next few, their motions were smooth.

A crackle when their feet crunched into the layer of dead leaves and pine needles indicated that they had stepped from the open safety of the lawn into the wooded area. No communication was needed as Addie felt Nora instinctively take things more cautiously.

Barely a few steps in, she swatted at a low hanging branch. "At my neck level and probably your face, there is a branch. I'm going to lift it and we'll both duck under it." Addie raised it up and felt Nora bend at the waist and waddle under it with her. She relished in the sensation of Nora holding onto her for support, but even more so, she felt the little victories when Nora loosened her grip to work around small obstacles more freely.

A series of exposed roots made for an interesting

hurdle that Addie found herself stumbling on. This time, Nora came to the rescue to help steady her. The sound of Nora's elated cheer at being the heroine made Addie's heart skip with joy. She had been a nervous wreck about the possible outcomes of the game, but so far, it was bringing them together as a team.

Nora stopped. "How do we know if we're going in the right direction?"

"That's one of the best parts of the game." Addie slipped behind Nora and leaned over her shoulder, bringing her lips in close to her ear. "Shh, if we're quiet, you should be able to hear the metronome."

"The rhythm of the ticking, I hear it."

"Can you tell what direction it's coming from?"

What felt like a couple of minutes passed, then she felt Nora reach back for her hand. Addie's index finger was separated out for her and guided up to point out a specific location.

"I think we ended up wandering too far to the right of where we were headed. We need to go left to get back on track."

"I concur with your assessment." Addie took her place by Nora's side again. "Shall we?"

Once again, they fell into a perfect synchronization as their bodies moved as one. Nothing delighted Addie more than when Nora took the initiative to periodically pause to get her bearings on the metronome's location. A little tug at the base of her shirt was the indicator that Nora had determined the direction they move in.

When the ticking became quite a bit louder than it had been, Addie got excited that they were on the verge of finding it, but a slight delay stopped them dead in their tracks. With the upper part of her body protected by her waving arms and the lower half by her extended, toe-first steps, it was unexpected when she bumped stomach first into an object. By the abrupt stop Nora made, she assumed they had just encountered the same thing.

For the first time since they started, Nora completely released her hold on Addie. "Oh, this is odd."

On her way to initially place the metronome, Addie had recalled passing by what she believed they just ran into. "It's an uprooted tree on its side. It's your choice. Do we go over, under, or around it?"

"Let's be adventurous and go over it."

"That's the spirit." Addie felt around until she came across a thick limb protruding from the trunk. She stepped onto it so that it was bearing the bulk of her weight, then repeatedly bounced to test the strength of it. She reached out for Nora, guided one of her hands to the limb and the other to the tree trunk above it. "This is your stirrup, and this is your saddle. Mount up on this side and dismount on the opposite. It's as easy as riding a horse."

Nora pulled away from Addie and after some shuffling sounds and creaking of branches, there was a crunching of leaves when her feet hit the ground. "Not quite as soft as a horse, but you were right, same concept."

"I only hope I can do this half as gracefully as you did." Addie followed the same instructions she gave to Nora. The jagged texture of the bark scraped against her skin and made sliding off rough. She imagined, though, that her jump down was slightly easier due to the few extra inches of height she had. Once down, an excited Nora, who was practically bouncing with energy in the hold she regained around her waist, greeted her.

"The ticking is so loud. I can tell that we're close."

"I think you're right." Addie grasped onto Nora's wrist and made a sweeping motion with it. "Lead us to your tree."

With hands clasped together and fingers interlocked, Addie followed a step behind as Nora took them in a zig zag pattern, sweeping the area until she narrowed it down to a spot in which she came to a stop. She felt Nora pull down, and when she came back up, the distinct shape of the metronome was placed in her hands.

"Can we take the blindfolds off now?"

"Yes." Addie tugged the tie down with one hand, so that it fell around her neck. She blinked as the dim light from the shade of the tree cover seemed blinding after having her eyes covered for so long. When she was able to regain sight that wasn't blurry again, there was a view of Nora, who had pulled her tie up, creating a headband to keep her long hair out of her face. "Beautiful." The word was already muttered before she realized she had said it aloud.

"As are you." Nora touched her finger to the bar on the metronome to silence it. "It's a fabulous game. I really love it. Where did you learn it?"

"At summer camp, one of my bunk mates was blind. Some of the girls teased her so the counselor had us play this game. She was my partner and together we beat out all the other teams. After that, the teasing stopped."

"It seems like this game has been beneficial to more than one person. I needed this. Thank you." Nora stepped in and wrapped her arms around Addie in a tight squeeze.

Addie pulled one arm out to return the embrace while still cradling the metronome. She took a deep breath, reveling in the subtle aroma of Nora's shampoo. "Do you want to try it again? This time I could set the metronome up at the edge of the lawn and we can work our way back out."

"I would love to, but it will have to be another day. I have a lot of work to catch up on. So much that dinner for me will be in the office."

"Work?"

"I still run my father's business remotely from the manor. It's something I had no interest in taking over when I was younger, but after he passed, it became a priority for me to keep his dream alive." Nora averted her eyes to the ground and pressed an acorn into the soil with the sole of her shoe. "That, and it was something I could do without ever needing to leave here."

"I'm sure Mr. Rosin would be proud as long as you're happy. How about a raincheck on the game for another time, then?"

Nora's smile reappeared. "It's a date." She turned and nimbly bounded away towards the manor.

A tiny chipmunk scampered timidly to the acorn and plucked it from where it was embedded into the ground. Addie watched him, amused by his twitching nervous actions, but when she shifted her position to redistribute the weight to her other leg, he took off running to hide in a pile of nearby brush.

"It's okay, little guy. I'd rather it be you who leaves upset with me than Nora, any day."

Chapter Seventeen

Knowing that the remainder of the day and evening would be void of contact with Nora, since she was hard at work in her office, made Addie's time drag. The only opportunity Addie thought might be feasible to catch a glimpse of her and say hello would be during the delivery of her dinner tray in her office. To be sure not to miss out on the task, she volunteered her time prepping for dinner in the kitchen.

With little to no experience in the kitchen, Lisa made use of her strength, mixing large bowls full of dough. She was also enlisted for the repetitive tasks of peeling vegetables, shredding blocks of cheese, and zesting citrus fruits. All her labor was well worth the effort when she could shed her apron and deliver the tray.

The directions to Nora's office were simple being that it was one door away from Gregory's. She had wondered what was beyond some of the mysterious doors on the main level and was anticipating what this room looked like. A general theme ran throughout the manor that was consistent with ancient times at varying ages of history. Therefore, it came as a surprise when Addie opened the door not only to the most modern of them all, but almost futuristic in design.

The long desk that wrapped around the room was a gleaming metal. The swirls of color in it gave the illusion that it was in a liquid state. The artwork and décor were strategically placed to make the room look like the interior of a spaceship cockpit. Sitting in a chair that looked like a replica of a pilot's seat in a rocket ship was Nora dressed in a feminine business suit.

Nora looked engrossed in her work project, staring intently at a row of monitors. Although she had to have known that someone entered the room, Nora didn't give any indication to her that she had. Addie opted to skip the cue and bring the tray to her desk regardless. It wasn't her intention to disrupt her busy workday, but she was hoping to at least get a quick greeting in. That idea fizzled out when Addie reached the desk and was faced with a row of faces staring back at her during a video conference call.

One of the men on a screen rattled something off in Mandarin. Addie was shocked when Nora responded back in the same language. Immediately afterwards, another man spoke in what she believed was German and again, Nora responded in the same native language.

Impressed by the proficiency of her verbal abilities, Addie would have been content staying and silently observing more of the meeting. It didn't last, though, as she was promptly ushered out with a wave of Nora's hand once the tray was placed on the giant desk.

As it neared the end of the day, Addie considered exploring some of the already discovered rooms in more detail, but while trying to decide where to head to, she found herself opening the case to her violin instead. She warmed up with some simple scales and octave shifts. Once her fingers were limber, she transitioned to full songs.

Not long into her practice session, Addie noticed the shadow appear outside her door again. This time, she didn't want to risk Nora escaping before she reached the door, so she continued to play right up to the moment when she hung her bow off her right pinky finger, and used her free hand to pull the door open. "I thought I heard someone out here. Are you okay?"

Nora was sitting cross legged on the floor with her back leaning against the wall on the opposite side of the hallway. "I'm so sorry. I didn't mean to interrupt. I just wanted to listen for a while." She stood.

"You can come in anytime and I'd be happy to play for you."

"Thank you for the offer. I would like that." Nora peered into the bedroom from the hall. "You finished setting up your room."

"I did." Addie stepped aside so that she could enter. "Come in and check it out."

Nora passed into the room and swept her hand across the bedspread. "I wasn't sure what your style was. I had only just met you when I ordered these decorations."

"You were on point. Blue is my favorite color."

The portrait on the wall caught Nora's attention. "I can't believe Gregory was careless enough to leave this picture in here after I explicitly gave him instructions to have the entire room cleared out." She tilted her head and narrowed her eyes. "On the other hand, he probably wanted to keep it hidden away in here. He despised having to see my mother in photos with my father." She reached up to grasp the bottom of the large frame and lifted to remove it from the wall.

"Actually, I asked Gregory to leave it up."

Nora looked down at the picture. "This was your decision. Why?"

"You look so content in the picture. When I see it, I can't help but ask myself what I can possibly do to get you to smile like that again."

"That's sweet of you. I'll put this back, then." Nora turned and held the base of the frame as high as she could to hook the wire cord around the nail.

Addie watched her attempt to rehang the picture, but after a few unsuccessful stabs at it, she came up behind Nora. She extended an arm around each side of Nora's and used her height advantage to lift the frame. Once in place, Addie continued to push on one corner and then back to the other until it was straight.

Still surrounded by her arms, Nora turned. Addie dropped her hands from the frame and placed them on either side of Nora's jawbone. Using her thumbs, she gently raised her chin up and lowered her own head to meet in the middle. She pressed her lips slightly against Nora's, leaving tiny pecks in a row along her bottom lip.

Addie lowered her hands. "I'm sorry. I probably should have asked for your permission before kissing you."

"Trust me, it may have taken me off guard, but it's definitely okay."

"Are there any particular boundaries that I should follow since I'm technically your employee?"

"I think it's safe to say that you don't have to worry about rules because I'm the one who makes them."

"Well, in that case, what would you like me to do, boss?"

"If you don't call me that, you can kiss me again."

"Anything you want, Nora."

Addie chose to place her hands on the slight curves of Nora's hips. She felt Nora's hands curl around her neck. Her fingers played around at the base of her hair. Their lips met once again, but this time she was delighted at how Nora deepened the kiss with more pressure. When every millimeter of space on their lips had been explored, Addie separated them open with the tip of her tongue. Their tongues had just made contact when the sound of footsteps scuttling in the hallway caused them to break apart early.

In the short time Addie had been staying at Rosin Manor, it was on the rare occasion that someone other than the two of them were in this wing of the building. The halls in this area were usually quiet and empty. By the questioning look on Nora's face, it wasn't a normal occurrence in her experience either.

Nora removed herself from their intimate bubble to check on the commotion in the hall. She stuck her head out the door and turned towards her own room. "I'm in here."

The maid rushed to the bedroom door and took a good deal of time to catch her breath before speaking. "I apologize for interrupting you, Miss Rosin."

"No worries, Francine." Nora looked around the room until she caught sight of the violin on the bed and motioned towards it. "I was just listening to some music that Addie was so kind as to play for me. Did you need something?"

"While cleaning your office, I overheard a message that was left on your work phone. A Mr. Lo wanted to schedule a last-minute conference call for first thing tomorrow morning, our time zone."

"Thank you for the information."

"I wouldn't have come looking for you if I didn't believe it was of the utmost importance." Francine clasped her hands together and cringed.

"There is urgency in the matter. I appreciate the effort you put into relaying the memo to me in a timely manner."

"Not a problem, Miss Rosin." Francine wiggled her fingers in the direction of the bed. "I will let you get back to your concert." She turned and her footsteps could be heard clomping away down the hall.

Nora lingered in the doorway. Her body inched slowly backwards out of the room, but her gaze looked longingly back at Addie.

"Go take care of your business call." Addie reluctantly waved her out of her bedroom. "It sounds important."

Nora smiled and blew her a kiss with her hand. "Have a good night. I'll see you tomorrow." She jogged nimbly away, barely making a sound as she left.

Addie sighed and placed her violin under her chin. "Looks like it's just you and me again." She started playing out a slow, old Italian love song.

Chapter Eighteen

Knowing that Nora would be starting the day off with an early business call, Addie made sure to wake up in the morning an hour before she usually would. The timing was perfect, she thought, when she stepped out of her bedroom and caught sight of Nora heading out of hers. She couldn't help the big goofy grin that she could feel spreading across her face at the sight of Nora for the first time after their kiss.

Nora marched down the hallway as if on a mission. Her arms swung at her sides, bent at an angle that looked as though she could take off at a jog or run if she moved her legs any faster. A nervous excitement rushed through Addie as she approached, prepared to meet for some sort of embrace, however brief it needed to be for the sake of Nora's work.

All too quickly the opportunity for anything that might have ensued was lost. Nora stuck close to the wall on the opposite side from her, turning her shoulder as if she were recoiling away from any potential physical interactions between them. A minor upturn of the corner of Nora's mouth was so trivial that any intentions of it being a welcoming smile were translated in Addie's mind to a nervous, shying away sort of grimace.

In a state of disbelief over the lack of what had just transpired, Addie turned to the direction

Nora had just gone in, to see if any indication of miscommunication was present in her departure. While she was hoping for a wave, a wink, or a genuine smile, everything was made exponentially worse by ending up face to face with Gregory.

"It's about time you got out of bed. There's a lot of work for you to get done today."

Addie wanted to swat him away like the annoying bug that she felt like he was. She tried to see over his shoulder if Nora was still in sight, but all she caught a glimpse of was a flash of her hair as she rounded the corner to the staircase. Had Gregory not been blocking her, she might have gone after Nora just to confirm that things were okay between them, but every sidestep she took, he mirrored. "What do you mean by a lot of work?"

"You do recall that you were hired to *work* here, don't you?"

"Obviously." She tried her best not to roll her eyes.

"Then I suggest you get started, because Miss Rosin has quite the list for you to finish by the end of the day." Gregory thrust a clipboard in Addie's direction.

This time, she didn't attempt to hold back on her opinion of his negative attitude by giving him a taste of it as she snatched the clipboard out of his hands. She looked at a sheet with an itemized list complete with boxes to check off next to each line. "What is this?"

"Odd jobs that need to be completed. The following pages have detailed instructions in case you can't figure something out. Although, if you truly weren't lying on your resume, then your comprehension level should be high enough to read and follow simple directions."

She flashed him a look that showed just how much he disgusted her and spewed out the most sarcastic tone she could manage. "I'm sure I can handle it, but thanks for your concern."

"If you think you'll have time to eat *and* get all those tasks done, I suppose I'll see you in the kitchen." He sauntered off, flicking his fingertips back at her on his way.

Not wanting Gregory to think that she was afraid of not having ample time to finish her chore list, she headed directly for the kitchen. Upon entering, she felt her eyes widen at the sight of the tray on the counter. Delivering it to Nora, even if the conference call had already begun, meant she had the prospect of just one hint that things were okay. She tucked the clipboard under one arm and reached out for the tray as if it were a lifeline.

Lisa's voice shot across the room. "That's not for Nora; it's your breakfast, Addie."

She stopped short, hoping that what she just heard wasn't true. "What about Nora's food?"

"I had to prepare it early and Henry delivered it right to her office so that it would be there in time for her meeting." Lisa pointed to the tray. "I heard you had a busy day, so I thought you might want something you could take with you if need be."

She lifted the lid and pulled out the bacon, egg, and cheese breakfast sandwich from the platter. "Thanks for the meal." Addie used the sandwich to wave her goodbye to Lisa.

The first line on the list of chores instructed that they be done in order, so she followed the directions which led her to a room in the same wing that her bedroom was located in. This one, just as hers had been, was filled with furniture covered over with sheets. The description of a particular sheet was referenced on the list, so Addie crossed the room to a giant one hanging on the wall. She gave it a little tug and as it dropped, a flood of natural light lit up the room.

After unhinging the latch, she slid open the double glass sliders and stepped out onto a balcony which overlooked the garden area of the yard. Addie leaned over the edge of the stone guardrail and took in the view while finishing up the last few bites of her sandwich. When her hands were free, and wiped clean from the melted cheese, she took a better look at what was in store for her day.

Scanning over the list, her mind swirled into a state of confusion as to why it was necessary to be given such a formal work log, when everything prior had been so casual. Looking back, she couldn't recall a single instance in which she either refused or didn't accomplish completing a task assigned to her. The checklist represented a lack of trust in her work ethic and she wanted to prove it wrong. Her plan was to get everything done and do it perfectly to prove that it wasn't necessary in the first place.

After tracking down Francine to get the necessary cleaning supplies, she swept and mopped the balcony. Even though it wasn't specifically stated in the instructions, she took it a step further and scrubbed down each one of the stone pillars of the guardrail for added measure. The work was tedious, but when she was finished, the sparkling clean space somehow enhanced the atmosphere of how the rest of the view appeared. The time to relish in the spoils of her labor were short lived, though, as she had to move on to the next project.

At the open stable doors, she came across Ruth treating the leather on a saddle. Ruth stood from her crouched position and wiped the sweat from her brow. "Addie, how's your morning going so far?"

"Busy."

"Oh, really, what are you up to?"

She pulled the folded-up list from her back pocket, unraveled it, and held it out for Ruth to see. "Take a look at this itemized nightmare."

"It's not as horrible as you're making it out to be. Many of these are simple tasks."

"Difficulty isn't the issue. Demeaning is more like it." Addie shoved the list back in her pocket. "I would have preferred to be asked, or even told what to do for that matter, instead of being given a step-by-step instruction sheet that seems so impersonal."

"Hey, if you want to trade, I'll gladly take over that list while you muck out my stalls."

She crinkled her nose up and made the gagging motion with her mouth. "I'll pass, thanks."

"That's what I thought. So, I'm guessing something on the list brought you down this way for a reason."

"According to the notes, there's supposed to be some sort of storage area in the barn."

"Follow me."

The second level of the barn was filled with equestrian equipment, most of which looked too antique to use. In the far corner, though, Addie caught sight of the two high backed Adirondack chairs she was searching for. The oversized chairs, paired with the solid hardwood they were constructed with, made pulling them out of the confined space awkward. Every step from one end of the sweltering, dusty barn attic to the other resulted in a cringe worthy bang to her chin from holding the chair at the wrong angle. Not wanting to waste precious time by stopping to readjust, she continued to the opening of the stairs, bearing the pain.

Peering down into the opening, she examined the precariously unstable looking steps. She didn't feel steady going up them, and certainly didn't trust descending with a bulky, heavy object in her hands. "Any ideas of how I can get these down without breaking them, or myself for that matter?"

There was a loud clanking noise as Ruth dragged a long length of chain on the floor behind her. The end in her hand had a large hook attached to it. She clamped it around the arm of the chair. "Head on down. I'll lower it over the edge to you."

Having a sizable chair dangling above her head, hanging by an old, rusted chain, was not Addie's first choice for getting the job done, but she didn't want to waste the time to come up with another plan. After the first one was safely on the ground, she unhinged it while Ruth went back for the other chair. The second attempt went much smoother, and they greeted each other with an enthusiastic hand slap when it was over.

"Any thoughts on how I might go about getting these back up to the manor?" Addie flashed her a big, gritted tooth grin, hoping that Ruth would see the blend of humor and seriousness she was feeling about the overwhelming chore.

"There's a pile of sandpaper on the shelf over there. Clean these up a bit so they aren't so rough.

They got weather-beaten, but the natural wood grains will look beautiful if you put a little elbow grease into them. While you work on that, I'll go hook up the trailer to the four-wheeler." Ruth hurried off.

The previous stain job on the chairs was badly worn and chipping off in sections. The sandpaper removed any potential dangers of splinters that might befall Nora, so Addie rubbed every inch of surface space until they were smooth. By the time she was finished with the second one, Ruth had already loaded the first onto the trailer.

Out on the balcony, Addie set down her side of the chair and arranged it so that it mirrored where they had set the first just a few minutes prior. "I'm not sure if recruiting your help is against the rules of the chore list, but I don't know how I could have done this without you."

Ruth let out a booming laugh. "Don't let the idea of the list get you down. And, no, we all work together here like cogs on a machine. If someone needs help, everyone pitches in to get the job done."

"Well, in that case, I appreciate the assistance with this one." Addie pulled the list and a pen from her pocket. She made the motion of dabbing the tip of the pen on her tongue and over exaggerated the checkmark she placed in the box next to the task. "I hate to run out on you, but I've got to get going if I plan on finishing this on time."

Ruth bowed her head, slid the door open, and signaled for Addie to pass through first. "Good luck to you, and don't forget to ask for help if you need it."

The next phase of Addie's workday brought her out to the garden. Her first experience there had been after dark and in a stealthy mode. It had been magical with all the little lights illuminating the space, but during the day, she could really see the bright splashes of color from the blossoms of the hundreds of different flower species. The statues, both looming and obscure, were easily noticed as well, compared to hidden in the shadows of night. It was a wholly different place that she would add to her ever-growing catalog of places to explore further in depth on the Rosin Manor property.

The intended destination in this area was the tool shed at the far end of the garden. Unlike typical sheds, it was designed to match the fantasy aesthetic of the area by being built in the shape of a castle. Addie could see the spires on the roof from a distance and headed towards it. When she got close enough to see the details of the trim work carved into the wood frame of windows, a different section of the garden caught her attention.

The tiny graveyard had been Nora's focal point the other night, but Addie had been more fixated on Nora than on the cemetery itself. She had seen the two headstones for Mrs. and Mr. Rosin, but hidden behind them she spotted a smaller one. She got close enough to read the dedication carved into the marble stone. It had the name Howard Jack Krane, a line about being Mr. Rosin's devoted business partner and friend, along with the date which matched the one the other two stones.

Noticing that the Rosin's each had freshly picked bouquets laid out in front of their stones, Addie searched the area until she found a bush bursting with yellow roses. She picked a few and nestled them into the grass against the memorial stone. Even with the time constraint, she felt compelled to sit on the stone bench for just a moment to pay her respects.

Addie took the position on the seat in the exact spot that Nora had been in. She wondered how many hours or even days in total that she must have spent in this location, mourning her losses. She turned and angled her head up towards the manor. There was a perfect view of the gravesite from almost every rear window of the estate. "Oh darling, Nora, it's impossible to heal from a tragedy when you can't turn your face away from it."

Fearing that the sadness of it all would begin to whittle away at her, Addie quickly stood and averted her attention back towards the shed. She grasped the door handle, which was carved to look like the hilt of a sword and opened to the most perfectly organized storage space she had ever seen. She passed by stacks of organic potting soil, rows of seed packets in alphabetical order, tools hanging on hooks, and pots on shelves. For a space used primarily for a hobby centered around dirt, there wasn't a speck of it to be found on the premises.

What she had come in for were the strings of tiny white lights which were strung up on just about every square inch of the garden area. They were also used to cover the entire outdoor staging area of the concert in the forest. They must be a favorite of Nora's and were bound to be stored in bulk amounts. At first glance in the shed, Addie thought she had come to the wrong location specified on the list, but upon closer inspection of the upper level, she found them.

In the gap just above her head, lining the space below the ceiling, were hooks evenly separated so that a wound up set of lights would fit on each one. She spun in a circle to confirm that there was indeed enough to fill every spot in the shed. Using an outstretched arm as a makeshift hanger, she looped one strand at a time until nothing other than wires and lights covered all the exposed skin. She could almost guarantee that if she were to come back to the shed in a few days, that every empty space from where she took down a set of lights would have a new replacement waiting.

Following the example of how it was done at other locations, Addie decorated the entire balcony. Tiny white lights were wound up and down every rung of the railing and across the top. She also created a frame of lights around the sliding doors.

So many were needed that she had to make a second trip to the shed for more. While she was there, she picked up a few citronella candles. They weren't on the list, but lights meant that the space would be used after dark, and that's when the mosquitos came out.

On her way back to the manor, she looked up at the progress of her work. Even in its unfinished state, Addie had fashioned a charming little space. She hoped that it would bring Nora joy to spend time in it.

Chapter Nineteen

With the end in sight of completing the list, Addie bounded outside to get to her second to last task. She was completely confused though, when she searched every corner of the garden and did not find strawberries growing anywhere. She clung to the handle of the basket she had brought with her, and marched from one plant to the next, only coming across flowers. Frustrated, she consulted the directions that were now a crumpled wad of paper from pulling them out of her pocket and shoving them back in repeatedly.

She skimmed down to the part that referenced the strawberries and then read the details slowly word for word. "*Vegetable* garden." She repeated the words a second time and scanned over her surroundings. "There must be more than one garden."

Just outside the flower garden gate, Addie took note of all the exterior places she knew of that couldn't possibly be the location for a vegetable garden. Her eyes passed over Rosin Manor, the stables, the garages, the forest, and the pond. She believed that when she had been to the outskirts of property on horseback, she hadn't recalled any sort of growth other than the perfectly manicured lawns and strategically planted trees. With precious time ticking away, she knew that it would be simple enough to ask someone where it was located, but the idea of not being able to find it on her own was maddening.

Her attention kept wandering towards the forest. While it would be absurdly impossible to maintain a vegetable garden, surrounded by thousands of wild woodland creatures, she knew the secret was held there. She focused on the opening to the path, and then it came to her. Addie remembered that Rosin Manor's property had hundreds of acres of space. While much of that was in the uncleared land, including miles of trail systems through the trees, the property had to include a much wider roadside frontage than there was perceived to be.

Narrowing down the options, the road eliminated one side, and two others were bordered by forest. The last side, at the far end of the lawn, was a giant hedge that started at the roadside and extended all the way to the tree line of the woods. Addie had originally thought that it was a border between Rosin Manor and the next plot of land. Given the expansive amount of acreage behind, there was a distinct possibility it extended farther to the side than she believed.

The walk covering the ground to the opposite side of the yard was exhausting, especially since she chose to speed across it at a fast pace. Along the way, she had passed Ruth on a horse, but she was determined to find it on her own, so she waved and marched by as if she knew right where she was headed. Ruth didn't seem like she questioned where she was going, so Addie took that as a good sign that she was on the correct path.

Standing towards the center of the hedge. Addie craned her neck from one direction to the next, only seeing a solid wall of green. She squinted through the branches and tried to stick her arm through, but it was so thick and lush with leaves that seeing to the other side was impossible. She took a step back and concentrated on the perfection of the trim job. Whoever oversaw cutting them must have a steady hand and a sharp blade to have the skills for that kind of precision. Everything was so pristine that she almost gave up and turned back, until a bird landed in front of the wall. The crow tilted his head, almost beckoning her to follow it, and hopped towards the wall until it disappeared into it.

Addie blinked and shook her head, thinking she must have imagined the whole thing. There was no possible way for a crow as large as that to easily enter such a thick bush as it just appeared to. Without taking her eyes off the exact location of where it entered, she rushed over to the spot. Expecting to see a bird sized gap in the wall, she gasped at the much larger hole that a human could fit in. She tried looking at the opening from different angles and was amused at how it was carved out in an illusion that made it appear to not exist unless you were right in front of it. One of the tricks to it was the second wall of hedge placed directly behind the opening, just as the one in the flower garden had to obscure the view of the interior space.

She stepped through the opening and peered around the corner of the hedge. Addie could feel her jaw drop open. "Oh my." For as far as she could see, there were rows upon rows of vegetables and fruits growing. There seemed to be an order to things in that the different varieties of plants each had their own section, but unlike the rest of Rosin Manor, there appeared to be a chaotic mess to the growth. It was wild and messy and beautiful all at the same time.

With the basket in hand, she started in one direction, crossed over to another area, and then circled back to where she began, barely covering any ground compared to the total amount of garden space there was to search. Even though she had found the correct garden on her own, without help, she could wander aimlessly for hours before finding the one fruit she was sent for. "If only this place came with a map."

"Don't need no stinking map when you know right where everything's planted in the first place."

The gruff voice that came from directly behind Addie made her jump and drop the basket to the ground. "Ahh!"

The hulking man towered over her. He glared down at her with fire in his eyes. "Are you stealing from Rosin Manor?" Spittle shot from his mouth and stuck to his scraggly beard.

She held one hand up in the air as if she were surrendering and used the other one to pull out the list from her pocket. While holding one corner of the paper, she gave it a rapid flick to unfold it single handedly. She held it out with a shaking arm for the man to examine, in hopes that he would take the letterhead, emblazoned with the Rosin Manor crest, as a permit of sorts. "I work here. At the manor. For Nora. Miss Rosin, I mean." She looked down at the dirty overalls he was wearing. "Oh, I met you once on my first day here in the dining room. You're Roger, right?"

"Don't remember. Figured you'd be gone by now."

"It hasn't been *that* long."

"Get out while you can, or you'll never leave." He started to lumber off away from her.

"Hey, I'm looking for strawberries."

"I saw on that paper you showed me. Headed there now."

Addie wondered how he comprehended what he could have possibly read in the short amount of time he had seen the list. She shrugged her shoulders, picked up the basket, and followed the grouchy man.

They approached what looked to be a large mound of earth. A thin line of smoke billowed up from the opposite side of it. Addie worried that the extremely dry weather they had recently sparked a brush fire in the garden, but as they rounded the hill, she noticed a stone fire pit. Hanging above it was a large piece of meat roasting over the flame. A scent of the savory barbeque wafted in her direction and it reminded her of how famished she was from running all her errands. "That smells delightful."

"Critters keep eating the produce." Roger fished around the front of his teeth with his tongue, picked something out with his fingernail, and spat it to the ground. "So, I eat them."

Addie tried to suppress the urge to gag. She focused on the space behind the animal carcass and noticed that this side of the hill was the front of a little house. A wooden door was propped open and there was a view of a bed inside. "Do you live out here?"

"Yup. Too stuffy for my taste inside that place." He nodded in the direction of the manor. "Besides, someone's got to protect the crops."

"I had no idea that all the fruits and vegetables that we eat were grown right out here."

"Enough to sustain us year-round. All the extras we donate to the food bank." He swatted at a fly buzzing around his arm. When he lifted his palm from his muscular bicep, the dead fly was smeared across his brown, leathery skin. "Lisa usually puts her order in the night before for fruits and vegetables. Odd that you were sent here."

"I know, right? This chore list just confuses me."

"Whatever Miss Rosin wants, she gets." Roger pointed. "Berry section is just over yonder."

Addie raised the basket over her head to wave a thank you to him on her way to the strawberry patch. He was a man of few words and apparently a hermit, so she figured she wasn't hurting his feelings by not leaving with a heartfelt goodbye. She thought back to the day she first arrived and was reminded of how Roger compared working at the Manor to being in jail. She imagined that even without the no leaving policy in effect, he probably wouldn't step foot off his large garden plot.

The strawberries were so plentiful that she could have stayed in one spot and picked enough of them to fill the basket so that it was overflowing. There was a specific purpose for these, though, to be fulfilled in the final step of the list, so only certain berries would do. Addie was careful to only pick the ones ripe enough to eat that same day. She gently laid each of the plump, deep red pieces of fruit in the bottom of the basket. Carrying her freshly harvested goods back to the manor, as if she were transporting a newborn infant, she made it inside without damaging the delicate flesh of the berries.

Her final step took her to the kitchen, but along the way, she passed by the open door of Nora's office. She slowed and examined the situation within. Nora was standing with a folder in her hand, but there was no headset or phone to her ear, and the monitors had text, but no conference call videos. Since the door was ajar, she didn't think it would hurt to offer some sort of greeting, no matter how brief it might be.

Addie leaned her upper body against the wide molding of the doorframe. "Hey, how's it going?"

For a split second, Nora glanced up from her paperwork, but went right back to it. "I really have to get these reports finalized and sent out as soon as possible."

She wanted to wish her well on her work and take her leave, but before she had time to say anything, Gregory stepped out from the other side of the room and blocked her from the doorway. He shot her a smug look and shut the door in her face.

Insulted and hurt that she couldn't be trusted to walk away on her own when turned down for simply inquiring about someone's day, Addie continued towards the kitchen in a state of disbelief. So many emotions ran through her that by the time she walked in the room, she either wanted to toss the basket across the counter or stand there and shed some tears into it. The options were both stripped from her, though, as Lisa whisked the basket away the moment she entered.

"There is a workstation with all the ingredients you need for your recipe over in that corner." Lisa pointed to the counter space in one section of the kitchen. "I'll set these by the sink, so you don't forget to give them a good rinse before using them. Oh, and when it's time, the burner on the bottom left is for you."

Addie groaned. "It makes no sense to me why I'm suddenly given cooking duties when I have absolutely no experience in the kitchen."

"There are simple step by step instructions and

I'm here if you need help along the way. It's a great introduction to learning."

"I don't doubt that I can stumble through this, but it bothers me that I don't know *why* I'm doing it in the first place. I get that I don't have a specialty yet like you all have, but I feel like my skills are better used elsewhere other than doing little bits and pieces of everyone else's job."

"Stop trying to read so much into this project. It'll drive you crazy. Did you ever stop to think that maybe Miss Rosin is trying to get to know you through giving you a variety of different assignments?"

"That seems like the strangest way of going about it." Addie let out a discouraged sigh. "Just when I feel like she's opening up to me, she puts even more distance between us."

"You, my dear, could not be any more wrong about that." Lisa pulled a strawberry out from the basket and held it up. "And this is proof." She set the berry in Addie's hand and guided her towards the preconstructed workstation. "Now get to it."

No matter what angle Addie looked at the situation, she couldn't come up with a scenario in which Nora avoiding her and giving her a load of busy work to keep her occupied for the day was considered positive. Determined to finish the last step of her list, she meticulously followed each measurement, temperature reading, and mixing step of the recipe. None of the process was enjoyable, though, as with each stage, she dwelled on the notion that Nora had made the decision that she no longer wanted to be with her.

Each one of the plump strawberries was dipped in semi-sweet chocolate and then drizzled over with stripes of white chocolate. A dusting of crushed red sugar powder brought out the little bit of red color from the end of fruit that was left exposed near the stems. She positioned the sweet treats in a circular pattern on a cold platter and covered it to keep them fresh.

Chapter Twenty

The shower that Addie took after her long day of chores helped clear not only the dirt from her body, but unclouded the mixture of thoughts in her mind. By the time she stepped out to dry off, she had come to a final decision. There wasn't enough time left to heal Nora of her phobia and therefore changing the policy on leaving Rosin Manor was not a possibility. She no longer had to worry about hurting Nora by walking away, since Nora no longer seemed to care about her.

She vowed to herself not to take anything except for the violin that was given to her as a gift. Pawning it would more than cover the money owed to Mason and hopefully there would be enough left over to pay for a place to stay until she found work again. Every detail of the perfect escape plan was devised, until she stepped out of the bathroom door into the hall and almost landed directly into Nora.

"Addie, how has your day been?" Nora's voice was soft, and she flashed a meek smile.

"Pretty exhausting after spending every waking moment working my ass off to get your chore list done." Addie dug through the pocket of her dirty jeans that were balled up in her arms and pulled out the crumpled paper. She had checked off every item with a wide tipped red marker for appearance's sake. After holding it momentarily, much too close to Nora's face to even read clearly, she ruffled it in front of her.

Nora grabbed it away. "What is your problem?"

"I just have the feeling that you've been avoiding me all day and to cover it up, you gave me a million projects to complete."

"Did you finish them all?"

Addie would have crossed her arms had they not been full of clothes. Instead, she gripped them close to her body. "Yeah."

"Good, then let's go see what you've accomplished." Nora started down the hallway.

Determined to stand her ground with her decision, Addie considered the idea of marching in the opposite direction and walking out. Three things stopped her though. First, it would be irresponsibly rash to leave without taking her violin and bag with her. Secondly, it was eating away at her, not knowing why she was being rejected from Nora after their seemingly pleasant kiss the night before. Lastly, whether she wanted to admit it to herself or not, there was a magnetic pull that drew her to Nora.

As they passed by the open door of Addie's room, she tossed her armful of dirty clothes and towel in. In preparation for the outcome she was sure would take place, she made note of the location of the violin case and her messenger bag.

Nora had led the way to the room, but Addie was appalled at how she stepped aside when they reached the sliding glass doors. Addie made no attempt to hide that fact that she was shaking her head in disappointment. "I can't believe you are so full of yourself that you can't even open a door on your own."

Nora placed a hand over the area of her chest

where her heart was located as if she had just been physically attacked. "I'm perfectly capable of opening my own door." She slid it open and stepped out. "I just thought that you worked so hard on it that you might want to show off what you've accomplished."

With darkness set in, the sparkling white lights dazzled the balcony in a glimmering brilliance. The two seats were adorned with matching folded quilts for added comfort or warmth. They were close to one another with only a small table between them to set a bottle of wine and the strawberry platter on. Everything was scrubbed so spotlessly clean that the outdoor area was like an extension of the interior of the manor. The space looked cozy and inviting, yet the concept of how it was built left a bitter feeling in Addie. "How about I fetch your laptop for you so that you can make another task list for me for tomorrow while you enjoy your new little oasis?"

"You've been working here for days now and not complained once about the work. Is it the list that has you so angry right now?"

"I've never worked off a list, and neither has anyone else here. It seemed like you were just trying to keep me busy and away from you all day."

"Well, yes, that was my goal, but not in a negative way like you appear to be taking it." Nora placed a hand on the back of the Adirondack chair and leaned her weight on it. "I knew that I was going to be tied up all day, setting up a new overseas account. Coming to me after every new project was not a possibility today. I thought I was sparing you from having to take orders from Gregory."

"When you put it like that, I guess the list does make sense." All the preconceived notions she had built were breaking apart in her mind, causing a swirl of confusion. Addie grabbed the back of her own neck to help ground herself and paced in a tight circle.

"Something else is clearly bothering you still."

"Every time I saw you today, I just couldn't help but get this weird vibe that you weren't very happy to see me."

"To be honest, I wasn't."

The words were like a punch to her stomach. She had read Nora's emotions correctly and everything she had worked towards with her was meaningless. "I'm sorry I wasted your time. I'm going to see myself out." Addie reached for the door handle.

"Wait. Please allow me to explain."

"You can spare me the details about how I'm not good enough for you."

"I will, because I don't feel that way at all."

"You don't?" Addie let her fingers slide off the handle.

"There were countless days where I can remember how lonely my mother was when my father pulled all day business deals. After the wonderful end to last night, I felt horrible at not being able to give you the attention I believe you were warranted."

"So, are you telling me that you were avoiding me because you felt bad about having to work?"

"Yes. I wanted to plan something special for us today, but I didn't have the staff to do it. They were busy guiding a tour through parts of the manor, preparing for an upcoming art gallery showing in which I will be lending select pieces from my collection."

"I completely missed all that." Addie pondered on how she spent much of the day behind the manor on the grounds or out on the balcony working.

"With the kitchen hard at work on refreshments, Gregory and I stuck in the office, and mostly everyone else greeting and guiding guests, there wasn't anyone else besides you to prepare the romantic surprise I had for us." Nora waved her hands at the balcony setup.

"All of this is for us." Addie cringed at her mistake. "I feel like a complete idiot."

Nora reached for her hand. "Let's put this ridiculous day behind us and sit for a while."

"Agreed." Addie interlocked her fingers with Nora's. She attempted to follow the proper etiquette protocols by offering up the first chair to Nora.

Nora playfully swatted her away. "Oh, please, let's eliminate the formalities when it's just you and I."

"In that case, I'll let you do the honors." Addie held the wine bottle out to her.

Nora examined the top of the bottle and the fancy device used to remove the cork. She fumbled around with it until it was firmly in place but looked as though she was struggling to get it to turn. "It just won't budge."

Addie leaned across and held the base of the bottle. "Use both hands to get more power into it."

After a fair amount of twisting and pulling, a loud pop went off as the cork released. Nora poured them each a glass and raised hers up in a toast. "Cheers to all the hard work you put in today so that we have a beautiful place to relax tonight."

Their glasses met with a clink that rang quite loudly in silence of the night. Addie took a sip of the bitter tasting alcohol that she knew likely cost more per bottle than most made in a week, and yet she would never acquire a taste for. She leaned her head back in the chair. "The stars here shine so much brighter than in the city."

"I've often thought about having the telescope moved out here from the tower just to see an unobstructed view of the sky without the windowpane in the way."

She sat up. "Give me a little time and I can recruit a couple of the others to help me get it out here shortly."

"We have all the time in the world for star gazing. How about tonight we just appreciate them with the naked eye?"

The notion of time struck Addie with a pang of sadness. Her time at Rosin Manor was running out unless she could figure out a way for Nora to allow her back again, just once. "Hey, can I talk to you about something?" She turned in her chair so that she was facing Nora, but as she did, she came face to face with a strawberry.

"Bite first, talk later." Nora held one of the chocolate dipped berries up to Addie's mouth.

The sparkle in her dark eyes was enough to captivate Addie into delaying the dreaded conversation. She took a nibble off the end of the strawberry, biting through the sweet crunch of the thin chocolate layer and hitting the tart center of the fruit. The mix of the two flavors made the perfect combination in the delectable treat. "Mm." She picked up a strawberry and brought it close to Nora's mouth. "Be honest, but don't judge too harshly. I'm not an experienced chef by any means."

There was an over exaggeration of delighted sounds and an elated rolling of Nora's eyes as she chewed the bite she had taken. "I don't know if I could really call this cooking, or even baking for that matter, but you did an amazing job at melting, stirring, and drizzling ingredients."

"That is a fair assessment." Addie laughed at her own inadequate skills. "Oh, you have some chocolate on your lip."

"Would you mind helping me with that?" Nora leaned over the arm of her chair and puckered her lips out.

Addie met her over the edge of her own chair. Concentrating on hitting the tiny speck of brown chocolate, she touched her lips to the spot and gently swept the tip of her tongue over it. "I think I got it all."

A mischievous look spread across Nora's face. She picked up another strawberry and smeared it on as if it were a tube of lipstick. "You may have missed a spot."

"My sincere apologies. Please allow me to get that for you." Starting in one corner, she made her way, a single petite peck at a time, across her lower lip. Afterwards, she followed the same pattern along her top lip, savoring the sweet flavor along the way.

"Thank you for the assistance." Nora used another strawberry to draw a chocolate pattern on the exposed skin that was generously offered due to the low-cut neckline of Addie's shirt.

She watched as the artistic lines were drawn, starting up at her neck and ending where the line of her cleavage began. "I can't reach any of those spots."

"It seems as though this time I'll have to help you." Nora touched her lips to the spot just below Addie's ear and kissed down her neck, across her collar bone, and down between the top of her breasts, swirling her tongue as she went.

Observing her every move, Addie reveled in the attention that Nora paid to the seemingly insignificant parts of her body, bringing them to life with a tingling sensation. "Best view ever."

Nora's face blushed when she realized that Addie was talking about her and not the night sky. "We should trade positions so I can experience this view you speak of."

Using the tip of her finger, Addie pulled the collar of Nora's shirt so that it uncovered a small patch of skin. "I don't have as much access as you did. Would you be okay with me removing this?"

In a lustful bliss, Nora nodded her head in agreement, but then shifted her attention to the glowingly lit balcony. "I feel like we're on display out here. How about we take this inside?"

Without needing to be convinced any further, Addie promptly rose and offered her hand to help Nora up. She followed Nora's lead into the manor, closing the glass door behind her. Although she had an inkling of an idea that they would be headed to Nora's room, a nervous excitement welled up inside of her at the notion of seeing her private quarters for the first time at such an intimate moment for them.

Upon stepping in, the room most certainly did not fail to impress in its grandeur. It was spaciously generous but broken down into smaller sections for a sitting area and study on one side and a bedroom on the other. As with every other room in the house, this one had its own specific décor theme that was ancient Egypt. Addie didn't want to break the physical connection they had just established, but it was difficult not to get lost in exploring all the gorgeous artwork. "You have an impressive collection."

"I'll give you the grand tour sometime." Nora guided her across the room. "For now, you'll just have to endure the sights of what you can see from the bed." She backed up to the edge of the mattress and hoisted herself up.

"Somehow I doubt I'll be disappointed." Addie climbed up on the taller than average bed, and slid in closer to Nora. Her attention was back on where they had left off out on the balcony. Addie lifted Nora's shirt up over her head and tossed it aside. She ran her fingers over the lines of her collarbone and into the cleavage made by the lacy mauve bra that covered Nora's breasts. "It's a shame we forgot the strawberries outside."

"You'll just have to use your imagination."

"I suppose I could try. Remind me again where the lines were."

"It started up here." Nora tapped the spot just below her ear, then dropped her body down so that she was laying sprawled out, as if offering Addie an open canvas to work with.

Addie dipped her head down and pretended to nibble at the spot as if there were something edible located there. "Mm, you taste just as sweet as the chocolate."

She sighed contentedly and ran her finger to the center of her chest. "The design came over here next."

Taking direction, Addie moved to the next location and followed the swirling path that Nora invisibly drew out for her. Eager to get to the valley between her breasts, she moved lower. "I clearly remember this part." She rubbed her thumb over the silky part of the fabric where Nora's nipple protruded beneath it.

A series of soft moans escaped from Nora's mouth. She reached down and unbuttoned the top of her pants. Using the free hand that wasn't wrapped around Addie's back, she made a motion that went from between her breasts, around her belly button, and down the front of her pants. "That's how the rest of it goes."

Addie made sure to spread a giant smirk across her lips. "Funny, I don't recall it going that far down on me." She tapped her finger on her chin.

"It didn't, but that's where I would have drawn it if we had been in here."

"Oh, I see." Addie winked. "I was headed down in that direction anyways."

Nora raised herself up on her elbows and kissed Addie. "Before you go, could you do me a favor and remove this so that I have something to gaze at while you are away?" She tugged at the front of Addie's shirt.

She obliged by pulling off not only her shirt, but also unclasped her bra and tossed it aside as well. Addie tested the give that the fabric of Nora's pants had, but her hand could barely move in the space under the zipper. "These need to go too." She assisted in sliding them off and slyly removed Nora's underwear simultaneously.

When she looked down and saw that she was completely nude a step earlier than expected, Nora shot Addie a cunning look. It only lasted long enough for Addie to get her face between her legs, for Nora's eyes to roll back. She dropped down to the mattress again, moaning in pleasure. "I wish you could be feeling what I am right now." Her voice was an octave lower than usual, and breathy.

Addie paused from using her mouth and continued the circular motion with her fingers. "I can make that happen, if that's what you'd like."

"Yes, please."

She wasted no time kicking out of the legs of her own jeans and slid off her underwear along with them. While skillfully continuing the motions of her tongue against Nora's clit, Addie glided her body lengthwise against hers in the opposite direction. She could feel Nora gently raising her leg. With the separation, there was room for Nora to reach the exact spot she had been yearning for her to touch.

For a moment, Addie halted as her breath caught at the sensation of Nora's mouth as it skimmed the surface of her clit. She had to will herself back to the matching location to return the gratification. It was well worth the effort to know that for every motion she made to elicit the sounds of pleasure humming from Nora, that it was reciprocated to her in a flurry of vibrations from Nora's tongue.

She fought the urge to give in to the orgasm that her body so desperately wanted to have. When Addie felt the squeezing of Nora's thighs around either side of her head, she knew it was almost time. She relaxed her muscles and rocked her pelvis against Nora's face. The muffled sounds of bliss emanating from Nora gave Addie the cue to join her in the harmonious release.

For a few moments, they laid in a tangled mess of limbs draped over one another in various directions. When the waves of rippling tremors subsided, Addie gracefully flipped directions and pulled Nora into an embrace, planting a row of kisses along the side of her face, ending at her lips. "Are you cold?" She ran her fingers along the surface of little bumps that had formed on Nora's arm.

"A bit." Nora suppressed a yawn behind a row of her fingers.

The duvet cover that housed the feather comforter within was a velvety gold fabric with intricate black stitching used to create the designs of hieroglyphic symbols that lined up in columns across the blanket. Addie bunched up a handful of the soft material and pulled it up and around the two of them. By the time she had them properly tucked in, she looked down to see that Nora was peacefully sleeping.

Addie blew out a contented sigh and nestled in against Nora. Her eyelids felt heavy from the long, busy day. From this spot, she could see two of the posts of the bed were in the shape of obelisks. She stared at them, trying to remember the history behind their purpose in ancient Egypt, when she joined Nora in drifting off to sleep.

Chapter Twenty-one

Addie slowly blinked her eyes open, still groggy from sleep. The unfamiliar surroundings gave her a jolt of panic until she recognized the golden comforter and recalled having fallen asleep in Nora's room. She could feel her own nude skin rubbing against the velvety softness of the fabric, and it triggered an elated flutter in her stomach at the thought of Nora laying naked next to her.

She inched her fingers over to the side of her that Nora was last on when they had fallen asleep. With her arm completely outstretched, she still did not feel anything other than silk sheets. The king-sized bed was spacious, though, and she could have rolled farther away. Addie sat up and was met with an empty pile of blankets next to her. She turned to the other side, wondering if maybe Nora had changed locations, having a preference to what side she slept on. Disappointed, she found that she was too close to the edge for anyone to fit in the thin space available there.

Using balled up fists, she rubbed the sleep away from her eyes then dropped back down into the sea of pillows and sunk into the memory foam mattress. In hopes that maybe Nora was just in the bathroom, she decided to wait a few minutes before giving in to the idea of having to get up without the morning kiss she had hoped to share.

The sound of the bedroom door opening and

footsteps approaching the bed brought a giddy feeling of joy to her. She popped up, ready to grab Nora and pull her down on top of herself. Instead of the beautiful woman with long black hair, it was an elderly woman looking back at her, wide-eyed in shock. Addie looked down at herself to see in horror that the blanket had slid low enough to expose her breasts. She quickly raised it back up and held it in place. "Did you need something, Francine?"

The thin white skin on Francine's cheeks turned a bright shade of pink. She held out one of the silver serving trays to Addie. "Delivery from Miss Rosin."

The tray would be too heavy to grab with just the one hand she had available. "Unless you want another viewing of me topless, you should just set it down on the bed, please."

"Oh, yes, of course, Miss." Francine set the tray down, nodded her head, and hurriedly scuffled out.

Once the door was closed, she dropped the blanket and turned her attention to the tray. Her first thought was that it must be breakfast, but the lack of a beverage made her reconsider her speculation. She lifted the lid slowly and a bed of crimson red rose petals overflowed onto the tray. Laying on top of the floral decoration was a folded note card with Addie's name emblazoned across it in a cursive calligraphy font.

The top half of the card was a note that read: *Good morning, beautiful. You looked so peaceful sleeping this morning that I detested the thought of waking you. I have a special brunch planned for us to share together in one of my most beloved places. Please come as soon as you finish reading this. I've only known you for one week, but it has been the most wonderful week of my life. See you shortly, Nora.* The lower half of the card had a detailed map drawn of the forested area of the manor's property with a red X marked on it.

Addie could feel herself grinning from ear to ear with elation. She massaged the side of her cheek as she reread the note a second time, relishing the sweet sentiment within its words. When she got to the part about the timeframe in which they had known each other, though, she gasped as she tried to comprehend the severity of the predicament she now faced. "It can't possibly be an entire week already."

Both living and working on site at Rosin Manor made the days meld together in a confusing jumble in Addie's mind. She tried to recollect major events that occurred each day from her time there and kept track of the number using her fingers. The first time counting, she hoped she was wrong due to the morning haze still affecting her brain. By the end of the second and third times with the same outcome of seven fingers sticking up, she shot out of bed in full panic mode.

Each one of her articles of clothing that she had stripped off and hastily discarded during their passionate encounter was strewn about both in the bed and on the floor. She scrambled around, shoving body parts into each item while simultaneously searching for the remaining missing parts of her outfit. When she was sufficiently covered, she scooped up the note, bounded out of the bedroom, and down the stairs.

Wasting no time, she flung the door to the kitchen open and rushed in. Addie took a quick inventory of the people in the room, but none of them were Nora. "Has anyone seen Nora recently?" She scanned the space, hoping for an answer but was met with a bunch of heads shaking a negative response.

"Nora was just beaming with happiness when she left here." A plume of steamy air escaped from the open oven door. Lisa shut it with one hand and set the soufflé on a cooling rack with the other. She raised a spatula to point it at Addie. "I told you the strawberries were a sign. You had nothing to worry about, now did you?"

"Actually, I have much worse things to worry about now if I don't find her in time. Which way did she go?"

"She took a basket of food with her and left with Ruth, so I assume she's headed toward the stables."

Not being concerned with the formalities of politely offering thanks or a proper goodbye, Addie took off at a speed inappropriate for an interior space. The second she hit the backyard, she accelerated to a full sprint across the grass, still damp with morning dew. The barn appeared small from the lengthy distance away, but she maintained a constant eye on it, hoping to see movement indicating that Nora was still there.

With just a few steps to go, she rounded the corner into the wide-open barn doors and almost ran headfirst into a horse. She came to an immediate halt and reeled herself backwards in an adrenaline rush of fear.

"Whoa." Ruth stopped short, with a horse on either side of her. "Maybe we need to put the reins on you to slow you down. I was expecting you'd show up, but not all crazy like this."

"Please, tell me Nora is still here."

"Sorry, but she left almost an hour ago."

Addie frantically unfolded the note and held it

out for Ruth to see. She tapped the spot marked with the X repeatedly. "How far away is this location?"

Ruth scrunched up her nose and tilted her head to one side. "Distance wise, it's not that far if it was a straight shot, but due to the winding trails that lead to it, it's at just about the farthest point on the property you can get."

"Do you have a phone on you, so that we can call and ask her to come back now?"

"Service is bad enough in the manor that we all connect to Wi-Fi just to use phones. Once you get out of range, there's nothing past the tree line. She won't get a message until she gets back to the barn."

"The four-wheeler is fast, though, so how long will it take me to get there?"

"True, but you can only get to about here on it." Ruth pointed to a trail that split off from an adjoining one. "From here on out, the trail is too narrow for the vehicle and you need to take the remainder on foot."

Addie groaned, her patience wearing thin. "How long are you talking in total to get there?"

"I'd say about forty-five minutes, give or take, and that's with the knowledge that Nora has of the trail system. Give yourself a full hour to be safe." Ruth let out a snicker. "Although, you could probably shave off a few minutes if you move as fast as you did on your way at me through the door just now."

The insignificant joke that Ruth rattled off went in one ear and out the other without eliciting a reaction from Addie. She was too concerned with calculating the numbers in her head and aloud for clarification. "An hour there, another one back, and time to explain everything to her. Once I add in the travel it takes to drive into the city, there's just not enough time."

"City?"

"I have to go." Against everything her heart was telling her, Addie went in the opposite direction of where she knew Nora was waiting for her and sprinted back to the manor.

In her room, she slung her bag over her shoulder and reached for the violin. As she did, her heart sank. Not only would there not be enough time to properly sell the instrument to someone who would pay top dollar, but even a pawn shop would be too time consuming at this point. She berated her own thoughts with curses at how negligent she had been with losing track of the days.

Amidst the chaos of trying to make a quick decision, a split moment of clarity passed through her thoughts. During some late nights when she woke and had trouble getting back to sleep, Addie had formulated a contingency plan. Little seeds of ideas were planted as she came across certain items or observed how things were run at the manor. The only problem was that every time she had finalized the details of what she would have to do, she also predicted the outcome, and that only resulted in pain and suffering for all involved.

With no other option in sight, Addie set the violin down and raced down the hall to Mr. and Mrs. Rosin's bedroom. It was only a short time ago that she struggled with the moral ramifications of taking one of the rings from the Rosin jewelry collection. Now, as she opened the box to remove the gun from its hiding spot, she shook her own head at herself for the crime she was about to commit.

Taking the stairs down two at a time, she stumbled at the bottom and bumped into the driver.

It occurred to her then that she never even learned the man's name in the week that she had lived there with him.

"Ma'am, I was instructed to prepare the four-wheeler for you. It is parked in the driveway in front of the garage."

"Change of plans, actually. I'm going to need a different vehicle. Can you please pull out the car? I'll meet you in the driveway in a few minutes."

"The car is too wide for the trails, and the tires do not have the proper traction for the terrain."

"I need a ride up to the gate." Addie sighed heavily. "I have the right to leave whenever I want. I know I can't come back once I do."

The driver politely bowed his head. "I'll meet you at the car."

Addie gulped as she approached the open door of Gregory's office. She could see him sitting at his desk and knew that once she stepped in, the chain of events, once set in motion, could not be undone. She wiped the sweat from her palms on her jeans and tried to calm the pounding in her chest with some deep breaths.

"Are you just going to stand there and stare like an imbecile?"

His insult was enough to fuel her into action. She stuck her hand into her bag and positioned the gun so that it was placed properly with the grip in her hand. Addie pulled it out and aimed it at Gregory. "Open the safe."

Gregory's face turned a ghostly pale complexion. He raised his hands up in front of his body. "Let's not do anything rash, now."

"I won't need to if you do what I say and make

it fast."

He pushed his chair back and shimmied sideways to the safe, keeping an eye on the gun the whole time. His hand was shaking so much that he had to restart twice. "I can safely assume that you want the money."

"Set it on the desk." Addie took stack after stack of bills and placed them in her bag. When she counted out exactly twenty-six thousand, she pushed back the extra stacks he had set on the table. "I don't need this."

"You're even pathetic at being a thief."

"That's because I'm not a thief, and I'll prove it when I get this money back to Nora someday."

"You won't have that opportunity. We'll have you locked up before you have time to spend that much money."

Knowing that if she didn't leave soon, his premonition would be right; she took off towards the garages on the side of the manor. When she rounded the corner of the driveway, she was relieved to see that the car was parked, running, and the driver was faithfully standing at the rear door waiting for her to enter. She headed towards the limousine but caught sight of Ruth and rushed over to her instead.

Digging in her bag to push aside the money and the gun, Addie found her scrapbook and flung it in Ruth's direction like a frisbee. "I need you to do something really important for me."

Ruth looked at the car and back at Addie with a furrowed brow. "What's going on?"

"I don't have time to explain. I just need you to make sure that Nora gets that book."

"What is this?"

"It's my life, or parts of it, anyway. Nora might never talk to me again after this, but I need her to know the truth regardless of what happens."

"After what?"

"I have to leave, Ruth."

"No, you can't. It'll break her heart all over again."

"I know, but I don't have a choice."

Addie took the note that Nora had written to her from her pocket and balled it up into a wad of trash and handed it to the driver. "Do me a favor and place this on the four-wheeler seat and leave it out so that Nora sees it, please."

He looked at her oddly, but obligingly took it from her. Addie waited a few seconds for him to get far enough away to get into the driver seat and lock the doors. The car was already running, so she threw it in gear and hit the gas, not slowing until she reached the gate. She stuck her arm out the window and punched in the code she had memorized days ago.

Luckily, no one had changed the code and there wasn't some sort of override to lock her in, as the gate rattled open. Addie glanced in the rearview mirror, expecting that someone might be chasing after her either on foot or in another vehicle. All she saw in the distance was Ruth and the driver still standing in the space where she left them. They were too far away to see the details of their faces, but she could imagine that they were a mixture of dumbfounded and angry.

Once the gate was wide enough to fit the car through, she released the brakes and sped out. As much as she hated herself for everything she just did to not only Nora, but all of Rosin Manor, it was the only option she had left for herself due to her own negligence.

Chapter Twenty-two

Addie could have easily dwelled on all the mistakes she had made from the first day she entered the gates of Rosin Manor, and even farther back in life, to put her in the dreadful position she was currently in. The ride was an important one, though, in which she needed to focus on the next steps to take in order to get Buddy back from Mason without harming either the dog or herself in the process. With the unpredictability of her old boss, there were too many scenarios to consider all the possibilities. By the time she crossed the border into the city, though, she had tentatively run through how she pictured dealing with Mason, and it wouldn't be easy.

After spending the week in a lush green environment surrounded by nature, driving through the industrial backdrop of the city created with concrete and metal left her longing to be back in nature. The smog and graffiti clung to her like an old habit that she regretted returning to. She shuddered to visualize what life behind bars would be like once she was caught for armed robbery and grand theft auto.

She turned down the street where Mason's house was located. Memories flooded back of walking those sidewalks daily with a package of cocaine hidden in her bag. She wondered how many lives she had destroyed with every delivery. There had once been a time in her life when she dedicated years of studying to the pursuit of saving lives. It made her nauseous to think that she may have aided in harming, or even worse, possibly taking a life.

Instead of pulling in the driveway and taking the risk of tipping him off that trouble was approaching, Addie parked down the street a few houses away. She needed three car lengths worth of space in order to fit the entire limo, which would have been challenging to fit in a tiny driveway anyway. The extra time that it took Addie to walk to the house gave her a few moments to formulate what she was going to say to Mason. She would convey that she just wanted the previously discussed trade of money for her dog, and none of the bullshit that Mason tended to add on to sweeten the deal for his own benefit. It was in this moment that the most convenient opportunity presented itself to her.

A pizza delivery car slowed to a crawl in front of the house and parked out front. Addie rushed to meet the driver before he had the chance to exit the vehicle. She tugged one of the bills out from one of the stacks in her bag and slipped it to the teenager with an acne covered face. "You can keep the whole thing if you give me your hat."

The teen nodded profusely and the gleam from his mouth full of braces shimmered when he grinned at the money in his hand. "One-hundred bucks?"

Addie turned her palm face up and waggled her fingers. "I don't have all day, kid. Hand over the pizza and hat."

He yanked the bright yellow hat with the logo bearing a pizza slice off his head and a greasy mop of curly red hair dropped around his face. "Here yah go, lady."

She glanced down at the dirty hat that smelled like teenage boy sweat and plopped it on her head before she thought too much about how disgusting it truly was. Addie snatched the pizza box from him. "Pleasure doing business with you, kid."

Addie pulled the rim of the hat down so that it concealed her face but made sure that the pizza logo was showing directly in front of the peephole of the door. She pressed the doorbell and waited with anticipation. Within seconds, an incessant barking began, and she let out a sigh of relief that her dog was still okay.

After living with Mason and John for far too long, she had learned their habits well enough that she knew they were currently going through the motions of their food delivery routine. Addie could picture Mason counting out the exact amount of money for the bill and adding only one extra dollar to the amount. With a measly tip like that for repeat deliveries, she was sure that their pizza must contain a certain amount of spit added as a bonus topping. She then knew that Mason would hand off the money to John, because he never trusted answering the door himself. Mason had claimed that it was beneath him to do such menial tasks since he was running the operation, but it was obvious that he was too scared that one of his clients would find him and off him to eliminate the competition. She also knew that he liked beer with his pizza and would currently be at the refrigerator getting a cold one out.

The door swung open and John held out the wad of cash. Addie pocketed it, but when John tried to take the pizza, she used the box to push him into the house. Since he was skinny and probably drunk, high, or both, and caught off guard, he was easy to physically manipulate back into the small kitchen space of the house. Luckily, Mason was exactly where she predicted him to be.

"What the fuck, dude." John tried to swing at Addie, but she used the pizza box as a shield.

"Calm down, it's just me." Addie pulled the hat off her head and stuffed it in her bag.

"Well, holy shit. Look who came crawling back to us." John took a couple of unsteady steps to the counter and leaned on it.

Mason closed the refrigerator door slowly, twisted the cap off the beer, and took a long swig from it. "I told you she'd be back for the mutt."

Addie's eyes followed a tiny whimpering sound that came from under the table where Buddy was tied to one of the legs by a short leash. "Let him go, Mason."

"Where's my money, bitch?"

"I have it all right here." She reached into her bag and flashed a few stacks of bills. "Let him go and you can have it."

Mason motioned for John to go untie him. "What did you do, rob a bank or something?"

"I got you the money you asked for; it doesn't matter where I got it from."

Buddy started to run to Addie, but Mason stepped on his leash and he got jerked back. "There's probably more where you got that from. I can't believe you're holding out on me after all I've done for you."

"I'm giving you what I owe you. I don't have any more. Give me my dog back."

"The price of the mutt just went up." Mason reached into the back of his pants but pulled his hand back empty. He looked confused and panicked and his eyes darted to the living room.

Without giving it a second thought, Addie reached in her bag and pulled out the gun, aiming it at Mason. "It looks like you left yours in the other room."

"Don't do anything stupid, now." Mason took a small step in the direction of where his gun was located. "You probably don't even know how to use one of those."

Addie pulled back on the hammer and placed her finger on the trigger. "Just ask the guy I robbed earlier to get the money in the first place."

"Looks like you'll have more than one bounty out on your head unless you pay me and leave now." He took another small step towards the living room.

"I plan on turning myself in after I get my dog somewhere safe."

"What's wrong with you? Only an idiot would do something like that." He progressed another step.

"Stop moving." Keeping the barrel pointed at Mason, she sidestepped her way to the coffee table, where his pistol was carelessly left. "I've already been told today that I make a pathetic thief." She dropped his gun into her bag. "I don't think I'm doing half bad, though."

"You'll pay for this."

"You have your phone if you'd like to call the police and let them know that your employee in your cocaine dealing business has gone rogue and stolen your weapon and drug money."

"Fuck you."

"That's what I thought. Now, unless you want to end this with a gunshot wound in one of the vital organs that I'm aiming at, I would let my dog go."

A drunken laugh escaped from John. "She told you off, dude."

"You let her in here, asshole. You'll be the one to pay when she leaves." Mason lifted his foot off the leash.

Buddy bounded over to her and scratched his front paws up her leg, begging to be picked up. Addie crouched while still aiming the gun and cradled her free arm for him to jump into it. He licked under her chin feverishly. Under any other circumstances, she would have repaid the welcome with a good scratch on the top of his head, but she just needed to get out while she was ahead.

Addie backed her way to the door, not taking any chances of dropping her guard. "It didn't need to go like this, but you got greedy." She took one last look at their dumbfounded faces on her way out the door.

Her feet hit the sidewalk and she sprinted the entire way to the car, where she yanked on the door handle, slid into the driver's seat, and pounded on the buttons until the locks clicked shut. She slunk down in the seat and held Buddy tight to her chest, peering into the mirrors to check if she was being followed. Only seconds passed when both Mason and John went running past the car, guns held down at their sides, trying to look inconspicuous, but failing miserably. Addie couldn't believe that they had rushed right by her without a second thought of looking, but then she remembered what kind of car she was in. They would assume she was on foot because she hadn't owned a vehicle a week ago when she lived with them, and they certainly would never consider that she would be traveling in a stretch limo.

She cautiously sat up in the seat. Neither of the guys were in sight, but when she looked in the side mirror, the tint on the window was so dark that she couldn't even see her own reflection. Confident that she could slip away unseen, Addie pulled away from the curb and started back towards Rosin Manor.

Chapter Twenty-three

With the uncertainty of what was waiting for her at Rosin Manor, the drive back was anxiety ridden at best. Multiple times, she hit the button to turn on the radio, but finding no solace in the music, she turned to silence, which did nothing to calm the chatter in her mind. Just as the events of the day were about to crash down on Addie in a frenzied mental breakdown, Buddy nudged her elbow with his wet nose. She glanced down at his excitedly panting tongue hanging out, and wagging tail banging against the seat. She patted the top of his head. Given the chance to redo the bad decisions she made throughout the day at the cost of his endangerment, she wouldn't change a thing.

At the gate, she lowered the window and entered the code. Even if no one were actively keeping watch, that alone would trigger someone to take notice of her arrival. She rolled slowly down the driveway, half expecting the entire staff of Rosin Manor to confront her. It also didn't completely surprise her when she got close enough to see that the sole person waiting there was Gregory.

Addie stepped out of the car with her hands raised. "I'm not armed." Buddy hopped out the car, faithfully following at her side.

Gregory still looked as flushed as he was when she left. The sweat stains under his arm   pits drenched through his dress shirt. "It doesn't matter if you are or aren't. I won't let you hurt Miss Rosin."

"I have no intention of hurting her." Addie reached across the seat to grab her bag. She held it out at arm's length by the strap. "Go ahead, take it."

He tentatively stepped just close enough to snag the bag out of her grasp. Then Gregory scuffled backwards to the spot he was in prior, as if it held some sort of invisible wall of safety. He peered into the bag and pulled out a handful of stacks of bills. "What is this?"

"All of the money is there. Well, most of it anyway. I needed a hundred for pizza and a hat." She pointed to the limo. "Oh, and I had to fill the tank back up. That thing is a gas guzzler."

"Am I understanding you correctly? You robbed Miss Rosin to go on a joyride and have an expensive lunch?"

"I only left because I needed to get my dog back."

"We offered to retrieve your possessions on your first day here." Gregory dropped the money back in the bag.

"Things were far too complicated for that and a danger to anyone who goes there. I had to do it on my own. I made things right, though. I returned most of the money and the gun too."

Gregory reached back in the bag and pulled out the pistol, holding it up by two fingers and looking at it curiously. "This vile looking thing is *not* Mr. Rosin's collection piece."

"Oh, I almost forgot about that. Think of it as a trade for the money I had to use. The other one is in the bag too."

His eyes glimmered as he set them on the correct

weapon. He pulled it out carefully and wrapped his hand around the grip. The bag was set aside at his feet as he used his other hand to steady the gun and aim it directly at Addie. "Now *you* will know how it feels."

Addie swallowed but her throat was parched. "This is the second time this week that I've been on the other side of the barrel of a gun. Trust me when I say that it doesn't feel any better to be the one holding it." She questioned whether she'd rather have an experienced firearms expert with an unstable personality, or a reasonably competent person with no clue how to properly handle a butter knife, let alone a loaded gun, pointing a gun at her.

A maniacal smirk spread across his face. "The control is kind of nice. I could get used to this. Now I can keep you in place until the police get here."

Addie could feel her heart heavy in her chest. "Nora called the police."

Gregory snickered. "No, I did, the second you left here. They came and I filled out a report and told them I'd call if you came back."

"Where is Nora?"

"Pathetic girl is still out in the woods waiting for you to come sweep her off her feet."

"Wait, she doesn't know I left yet?" Addie instinctively started to move towards the side of the manor driveway where the four-wheeler was still parked.

"Stop!" Gregory waved the gun erratically in her direction. "Move another inch and I will shoot you."

She obeyed his command, freezing in place and raising her hands in surrender. A pang of regret at having handed over the weapons to Gregory too soon overcame her. "You claim to have her best interest in mind, but can't you see how badly this will hurt her?"

"Miss Rosin has only known you for a week. She'll get over you soon enough once she finds out how you've betrayed her trust."

A rush of anger boiled up in her. Addie knew that if she only had the opportunity to explain what happened, Nora might be understanding of the situation. "I don't think you really want to hurt me, Gregory." Addie took the risk and made a move towards the four-wheeler.

A shot went off. The sound was deafening in the quiet solitude of the manor grounds. A shocked Addie came to a grinding halt. She took a personal inventory of her own body, uncertain if any little ache or pain in her body could potentially be a fatal wound. When everything appeared to be secure, she frantically scanned the area for her dog. She let out a sigh of relief when she caught sight of him chasing a butterfly in circles on the lawn. Lastly, she looked to Gregory in disbelief that he would be bold enough to take a shot at her.

His face was flush and his eyes wild, darting from one place to the next. Beads of sweat dripped down his face. "I told you to stay put. This time I might just put a bullet in you."

"What was that loud bang?" The sound of Nora's voice brought everyone's attention in her direction, including Buddy, who bounced over to her excitedly as she came around the corner of the manor. She looked at him curiously and bent to give him a tap on his head. When she looked up to see the rest of the scene before her, her eyes widened. "What is going on here?" She started towards Addie.

"Miss Rosin, stay away from her, she's dangerous." Gregory flailed his arm, trying to flag Nora to go behind him.

Nora looked like a deer caught in headlights as she looked from one to the other. "Why do you have a gun, Gregory?"

"To protect you." He pointed at Addie like a child telling on another one. "She robbed me at gunpoint. Stole thousands from your safe."

"Is what he's saying true?" Nora's voice shook.

"Well, yes, I did, but please let me explain what happened." Addie tried to maintain eye contact with Nora for the opportunity to plead her case.

Gregory's voice broke through. "Not only that, but she car-jacked your limousine right out from our yard and left with it."

"You left the manor property?" Nora looked on the verge of tears.

"I did, but please just hear me out." Addie wanted to run over and kneel at her feet to beg for forgiveness, but she didn't want to risk Gregory's unpredictable trigger finger, especially in the presence of Nora.

"I can't believe after everything we shared last night that you could betray me like this."

"I didn't have an option, but I promise that I had planned to talk to you about this. Time got away from me and I messed up."

"Speaking of time, you left me waiting for you for hours." Nora held her hand out and opened her fingers to reveal the balled-up note card. "Don't worry, I got your message, loud and clear." She turned and started towards the manor.

Addie fought for the words to apologize, but before they could come to her, a siren sounded at the top of the driveway. She craned her neck in the direction of the gate to see blue lights flashing.

"Well, it looks like your ride out of here has come to get you." Gregory spat out a cross between a laugh and sneer.

Addie watched as Nora disappeared behind the front door of Rosin Manor. From that point on, everything else was mostly a blur. She could hear the officer yelling out to her to keep her hands up. She could feel the pavement digging into her knees as she knelt while being handcuffed. There was a list of rights being spattered off to her, but they went in one ear and out the other without the information being retained.

At some point during her arrest, Addie saw Ruth approaching. "Ruth, please take care of my dog, Buddy."

She didn't get to hear a response back, because the officer placed a hand on the top of her head and guided her down into the back seat of the patrol car. She complied with all the demands that the officer barked out, never once struggling or talking back. It seemed pointless for her to fight back, when there was no denying that what she did that day was illegal. With no funds to pay for a lawyer, she was at the mercy of the court system to decide her fate, and she didn't want to give them anything to hold against her.

She watched through the bars separating the backseat of the cruiser as her bag, still filled with the money, and both guns were confiscated as evidence and placed in the front. She watched as Gregory animatedly motioned to the items that were taken and then again pointing to the manor and the gate. Without hearing any of the conversation, it was obvious that he was concerned about getting the money and Mr. Rosin's gun returned. Addie also wondered if he was being summoned to the station to fill out a report and trying to explain that he couldn't leave. If he were forced to, Addie wouldn't feel any remorse for him, but it destroyed her to think how it might affect Nora.

As they pulled away, Addie pressed her forehead against the window, arching her neck, trying to keep the manor in her sights. She hoped for a glimpse of Nora in one of the windows, but at least the visual of the outside of the historic building would be etched in her memory.

She watched the trees as they flew by in a green blur outside the window. It triggered an uneasy motion sickness in her gut, but the idea that this might be the last time she would enjoy the views of nature before spending time behind bars gave her the will to push through the nausea.

The trees began to thin as they transitioned from the country setting into the village of the small town. It was a quaint area filled with local businesses instead of retail chains. They pulled into a tiny police station that appeared to be attached to the fire department as well as the town hall. The common area across the street was outfitted with picnic tables, swing sets, and a little white gazebo in the center. Humiliated at being removed from the back of the police cruiser in handcuffs, she bowed her head away from families curious about the strange criminal invading their small town.

Once inside, the embarrassing moments continued throughout the booking process, as she endured a more intense body search than the one given to her on site at the manor. She was administered a breathalyzer test and had to supply a urine sample under a watchful eye. Unlike the application form she filled out with minimal personal information supplied, her true identification was recorded. Even though her criminal background check came back clear, she was still fingerprinted and had her mugshot taken.

When the entire grueling process was complete, she was locked up in a holding cell for what she was told would be for approximately forty-eight hours until a hearing, where a judge would determine if she was eligible for bail. Addie had joked with the officer that unless she could use the money in the bag they had confiscated from her, there was no way she could post bail. It elicited a tiny grin and a head shake, but that was as much conversation as she deemed necessary until she could figure out what her legal rights were.

The cell gave her an immediate feeling of being confined, which slowly progressed into being choked as the sensation of claustrophobia seeped into her every thought. Recognizing the anxiety-based reaction she was having to the idea that she might be spending years trapped in a similar space, she tried to have a more optimistic outlook to get her through the next day at least. To start, she focused on how grateful she was that they arrested her in a small town instead of the city where she would be stuck in a holding cell with other recently booked people.

With nothing else to do but stare at the ceiling while lying on an uncomfortable cot, she began to wonder if Ruth gave Nora the scrapbook. She pictured Nora going through the pages and learning all the truths that she had concealed from her.

Chapter Twenty-four

The clanking of keys banging against the metal bars woke Addie from the sleep she felt like she had just settled into. She sat up on the cot, and scratched where the abrasive material irritated her skin. Then she rubbed at the sore spots where the metal bars creating the cross support of the flimsy makeshift bed had dug into her back. She shook her head at how often she went from good to bad and back again repeatedly in her life.

A different officer than the one who had arrested her yesterday slid the cell door open. After getting in the habit of following the correct protocols, Addie rose slowly, approached the door, turned, and placed her hands behind her back in preparation for the handcuffs.

"No need for that."

Addie turned, confused. "Am I going to my bail hearing, or being transferred directly to the county prison?" She had heard a rumor that if a crime was too severe or she posed a danger to others, then bail wasn't even offered as an option. She didn't think that what she did was violent enough to condone such a harsh penalty, but then again, Nora Rosin was probably the most high-profile member of the community, and Addie had done her wrong.

"Neither. You're meeting with your lawyer."

She knew little about law, having only taken a

political science class to satisfy a core requirement in college. "Is this the one that the state is appointing to my case?"

The cop shrugged, causing his slightly too tight uniform to pull the buttons on the front of his shirt to the limit before risk of popping. "Not my duty to keep track of where they come from. Just my duty to take you to them." He motioned for her to go in front of him. "Down the hall, last door on the left in the conference room."

Addie went to where she was directed and turned to the officer for the official confirmation that it was okay for her to open the door. She took his slight head nod as an acceptable response, still being cautious not to break any more laws than she was already paying for with her lack of free will. She barely had one foot stepped in the room when a woman with dark curly hair sprinkled with gray strands hopped up from her seat to greet her.

The woman extended her hand out to shake. "Adeline Krane, it's a pleasure to be working with you. I'm Rebecca Parker, your attorney."

She wasn't sure whether it was stranger to be addressed by her formal name for the first time in years, or to have such an aggressive lawyer to be appointed to her case, considering the horror stories she had heard about lackluster efforts of court appointed legal representation. She returned the greeting with a solid handshake. "So, you've been assigned my case?"

"If by assigned you really mean hired, then yes."

"Are you one of those pro bono lawyers?"

"While it is valiant for those who offer their time for free, I assure you, I am being paid exceptionally well for my time."

"A lack of money is how I got myself in this situation in the first place. If you expect to get paid for your services anytime soon, I'd pick a new client."

"Nora Rosin has paid in full for me to represent you."

"Call me crazy, but I'm slightly leery of trusting legal help from the person I'm going up against in court."

"Quite the opposite actually. Miss Rosin is aiding you in your allegations against Mr. Gregory Webster." Rebecca pulled a chair out from the conference table. "Have a seat and I can update you on exactly what we are dealing with here."

Addie slid into the hard, plastic chair. She was confused by the exchange she just had with the woman who claimed to be her lawyer, but for the first time in the last twenty-four hours, she didn't feel completely hopeless. "Don't sugar coat things. Tell me exactly what I'm dealing with here."

Rebecca pulled a manila folder out from her briefcase and flipped it open. "Considering that the initial statement Mr. Webster filled out had you suspected of armed robbery and grand theft auto, things are greatly improved."

"I don't understand. What changed?"

"First of all, at the time of arrest, you had brought the vehicle in question back to Rosin Manor. This automatically changes the charge down to an unlawful taking of a vehicle, since your intent was shown to eventually return the car to the owner."

"So, basically it dropped from a felony to a misdemeanor."

"Exactly." Rebecca pointed a finger into the air. "It gets better, though."

"The money. I gave that back too." She thought about the hundred dollars she used to buy the pizza and hat. "Well, most of it, anyway."

"True, when the police arrived, it was in Gregory's possession. The important part of the entire case, though, is that neither the car, the gun, nor the money belong to him."

"Yet, he's the one who filled out the police report."

"Precisely." Rebecca flipped the page in her folder. "According to a statement by Nora Rosin, she is claiming that you were told that you could have the money and given permission to use the car. Due to a negligence on her part to communicate to Gregory that you were given the okay to take the vehicle and money, you may have resorted to extreme measures to obtain the items."

"Nora actually said those things?"

"Wrote them out and signed them, first thing this morning when she hired me."

"I don't understand why she would do this."

Rebecca flipped the page again. "According to the statement, in exchange for work done at Rosin Manor, she was offering to pay the debt of your college loans." She pointed to a figure on the paper. "The sum of twenty-six thousand was to be given to you for a week's worth of employment. You were borrowing the car to look into ways of creating an account to pay off the debt to Harvard University."

A shocked Addie spun the page around to see for herself that Nora's signature was indeed signing off on the testament. "So, where does this leave me now? You know, involving being locked up and all?"

"Technically, it is just a matter of pointing a gun

at Gregory, which is an assault charge."

"That's still serious, though, right?"

"Yes, but it is much easier to deal with a simple he said, she said assault charge when there was no physical evidence and you have a clean record with no prior convictions."

"Do you think I have a chance at actually winning this case?"

"Yes, there is a solid possibility, especially if you play the misunderstanding under dire circumstances card, but I have one other option in my arsenal." Rebecca licked her fingertips and made a flashy show of dramatically flipping the page. "I'm sure you are aware that there was a second weapon in your possession."

Addie gulped. "Uh huh."

"The pistol is registered to a Mason Conant." Rebecca pointed to a long list printed on the sheet. "This guy has a record a mile long. There are a lot of possession charges and the courts have been trying to catch this guy for something big enough to bring him down for good."

"You want me to help with that."

"It would be a perfect bargaining tool if you were up to the challenge."

"Possibly, if it would help clear my name."

"Tell you what, I will write this up in a couple of different ways and when it's time, we can go at it however you choose." Rebecca straightened out the stack of papers, closed the folder, and stuck it back in her briefcase. She extended her hand out to Addie. "It was a pleasure meeting you, and I look forward to representing you the best that I can."

"How do I contact you if I need to?"

Rebecca slipped her a business card. "I'll be in touch with you for the next step of the process. Got to run for now, though." She rushed out of the room.

Addie stood and awkwardly took the few steps towards the door. She opened it slowly and peered around the corner. "Hello?"

The officer who had escorted her in was standing guard just outside the door. "Are you ready to go?"

"Back to the cell here, or am I being transferred to a different facility?"

"To the secretary to fill out paperwork."

Addie rolled her eyes at the idea of more stuff to fill out, but anything was better than the giant cage furnished with the bed of metal. Once again, she led the way, coached with step-by-step directions from the cop. The desk where she was placed was vastly different than the one at booking time when she was handcuffed to the metal desk.

A woman with a beehive hairdo that she probably never changed styles from since the nineteen-sixties slid a stack of papers across her desk and pointed to a spot at the bottom of the top page. "Just sign on the line." She smacked a mouthful of gum.

"Before I do, I think it's best to have my lawyer look over these." She slid the business card to the woman. "This is her number that I think I have a right to call since I haven't used my one call yet."

"The one call rule is designated for at the time of arrest, and to be honest, it's really just a Hollywood myth. If you'd like to contact your lawyer now, you can, but this paperwork is for your release. The sooner you sign it, the quicker you walk out that door."

"Release?"

"While you were in with your lawyer, a Mr.

Gregory Webster came in and issued a statement revoking his claims of you assaulting him with a deadly weapon."

"Gregory came here?" Addie pointed to the chair she was currently sitting in.

"Yes. Now, that doesn't mean you won't still have to appear in court. Due to this whole fiasco involving the police call and arrest, a judge will have to clear you for all crimes committed. Although, you are free to go since Nora Rosin just paid your bail money in full."

"Just?" Addie slid to the edge of her seat and gripped the arm rests. "Did she have Gregory pay while he was here, or did she call in the payment over the phone?"

"She wrote the check out to me in person."

Addie stood and hovered over the paperwork. "If I just sign here, can I go now?"

"Well, we need to get your personal items out of lockup and back to you."

She scribbled her name out and dropped the pen down. "I could care less about whatever you have."

Chapter Twenty-five

Addie pushed through the heavy door to the police station and rushed outside. From the top of the concrete steps, she scanned the area until she caught sight of the shiny black stretch limousine. She bounded down the steps, practically falling out of her sneakers, which had the laces removed during her booking process. Straining to see past the traffic traveling on the street and the playground equipment in the park, it was difficult to tell if the limo on the opposite side was stopped temporarily due to a red light or stop sign. Taking no chances of losing it, she put all her energy into sprinting in a straight line for the car.

Not bothering to wait for the oncoming traffic to give her the right of way on the crosswalk, she saw an opening between cars that she could navigate through. Her erratic decision to dash in front of the cars elicited a beeping horn, which made her leap to the curb and stumble onto the grassy area. Without missing a beat, she continued across the park, not caring that she was interrupting someone reading a book on a quilt, a couple picnicking at the tables, a woman stopping to smell the flowers, and a child at play on the swings. Someone yelled out an obscenity as she hurdled the leash of a dog, but she continued until she reached the car.

Fearing that it could pull away at any moment,

Addie grasped onto the handle of the backdoor of the limo, securing that she had a hold of it somehow, no matter how fragile the connection might be. She leaned her other arm against the hot surface of the car and used it to support her forehead as she heaved gasping breaths in and out. She ignored the pain from the heat-soaked metal of the car on her skin, choosing the relief from not having to hold herself up over the burning sensation on her arm.

When the risk of her passing out from breathing heavily had subsided, Addie pulled up on the door handle and hopped in the back of the limo. Confused at the sight of the wide empty seats all around her, she gritted her teeth together as she wondered if maybe she just entered someone else's car by accident. The sound of the divider separating the front of the car and the passenger section sliding down brought her wide-eyed attention to who she might have just trespassed on. She held her breath at the idea of how embarrassing it would be to get arrested moments after just being released for stealing a ride in a stranger's limo.

Much to her relief, the face looking back at her was the driver from Rosin Manor, although she embarrassingly still hadn't learned his name. "Hey there." She waved awkwardly.

The driver looked nervous. "Is it your intention to take the car right out from under me again? Because if so, I'll need to make arrangements to get Miss Rosin back to the manor another way."

She glanced around a second time at the empty seats. "Where is Nora?"

"You passed her, and all the others for that matter, when you tore through the park like a maniac."

Addie scooted closer to the window and peered

out. If she hadn't been so fixated with getting to the car before it drove away, she would have noticed that it had been parked on the side of the road at a meter the whole time. She would have also noticed that it was Lisa and Henry with a spread of food at the picnic table. It was Gregory with his face in a novel on a brightly colored quilt. The woman enjoying the flower garden was Francine. The dog who's leash she came close to tripping on was her very own Buddy, Ruth walking him. The most important one, though, was the woman that she completely ignored, thinking that she was some random kid.

Addie stepped out of the car, feeling like all eyes were on her after she completely mortified herself during her mad dash out of the police station. She sheepishly made her way across the lawn, which, even though it was nicely groomed by public standards, looked like a jungle compared to the golf course perfection of the grounds of Rosin Manor. A section of the park where the playground equipment was located was covered in a red mulch. Addie stepped onto the soft substance and made her way to the large metal A frame structure that held two swings.

She was only a few feet away, and Nora still hadn't looked up at her. Nora's body was hunched over in the swing seat, dark hair falling around the sides of her face, obscuring it from view. Her feet dangled down just far enough to use the tips of her shoes to move her in a slight swaying motion. It made Addie's chest feel tight with regret for causing enough turmoil to make her look as broken as she did now.

Addie approached the empty swing next to Nora. "Is this seat taken?"

"It's a public park." Nora didn't look up from the

ground, which was heavily grooved from children's feet sliding through the dirt. "If there's no one in it, I can't stop you."

"I guess I deserve that." She slunk down into the hard rubber seat.

"You robbed Gregory at gunpoint, stole thousands of dollars from my safe, and hijacked my car."

"I'm not proud of the horrible things I did to you."

Nora reached into her pocket and pulled out a newspaper clipping and handed it over to Addie. "So, Adeline Krane, I can only assume that because our fathers were business partners, you intended on stealing from me all along, even before you got to Rosin Manor?"

She unfolded the article detailing the plane crash that claimed the lives of not only the Rosins, but Addie's father as well. "Ah, I see Ruth gave you the scrapbook." Addie cringed at the stark reality behind the accusations. "And, yes, that was my intention."

"Then why didn't you get it over with on the first day? I mean, just about every item in that house is worth more than the amount of money you took."

"That was my original plan."

Nora used the chains of the swing to pull herself up off the seat. She flung her hair over her shoulders and stood up in front of Addie. "How could you be so cruel as to stay long enough to make me fall for you?" She pulled the crumpled note from her pocket and held it up. "To leave me like this is just heartless." She tossed the note so that it landed in Addie's lap and placed her hands on her hips, glaring with glassy eyes.

She held the piece of paper up. "I knew this would hurt you, and that is exactly why I did it."

A quiet whimper of pain escaped from Nora. "That's what I was afraid of hearing. I never should have come here." She turned and started to walk away.

Addie scrambled to get up from the swing, and softly touched Nora's arm from behind. "Nora, wait. In the week that I've known you, I found that you tend to run away from everything."

"I'm confused. Do you think that insulting me is going to make me want to stay?"

She rounded Nora's body so that they were facing one another again. "I knew that the only way that I would ever be able to see you again would be to do something that would hurt you so badly that you had no choice but to chase after it instead of running."

"Yeah, well, you succeeded. I did exactly what you thought I would. You got me to leave Rosin Manor. Are you happy with yourself?"

"You, Nora, are the reason why I didn't leave that first night, or any of the other times I thought about it. I realized that I needed to find another solution to my problems because I didn't want to leave you."

"What was I, a project for you to try and fix? Don't you get that I can't be fixed?" Nora motioned her hand in a wave across the park that encompassed all the staff members from Rosin Manor. "They've all tried, but it didn't work."

"If there's anything I've learned this week, it's that I'm the one who's broken, not you."

"You?"

"While you successfully kept up with running your father's business, I dropped out of med school to become a drug runner because I didn't have my dad there to financially support me."

"I locked myself up in my house for seven years."

"Out of a love that you had for the people still in your life." Addie held up the crumpled note. "For the first time since the plane crash that destroyed both of our families, I felt like things were going to be okay, when you gave me this." She pointed to a spot on the map that was marked with the red x. "I promise you, if Buddy wasn't in the hands of a dangerous person threatening his life, I would have been there."

Nora watched Ruth jogging across the other side of the park with Buddy at her side. "I saw the photo in your scrapbook with your father and Buddy. He was your father's dog."

"Yeah, my stepmother hated animals and he wasn't worth anything of monetary value, so Buddy was the only thing of my dad's that she let me have." She took Nora's hand. "You have an entire museum's worth of family memories. Please understand that he's all I have, and I needed to get him back at all costs."

"I would have done exactly as you did." There was no hesitation in Nora's response. "I do wish you would have talked to me first. There must have been some way to better handle this entire situation."

"That was my intention, but to be honest, I was careless and lost track of the days. Time flew by as I was falling for you more and more. It wasn't until I was reminded in the note you left for me that a full week had passed since I had come to the manor. I could have lost him forever." Just saying the words aloud brought an icy feeling to Addie's chest.

"Hey, you're trembling." Nora rubbed the top of Addie's hand.

"Ah, yeah, the food options behind bars are not what I consider to be ideal."

Nora pointed to the picnic table covered with

a spread of food. "Lisa packed our lunch to go today. Come sit with me and have a bite to eat."

Before they even reached the table, Lisa and Francine were up and had switched modes from a relaxed pair on an afternoon outing to full-service employees buzzing about, prepared to work. They promptly created two place settings complete with cloth place mats, napkins, dishes, and silverware. Freshly squeezed juice was poured into travel tumblers and garnished with orange slices. Lisa started to scoop a spoonful of fruit salad onto a plate.

Nora reached for the bowl. "Please allow us to serve ourselves. I'd like for you to enjoy the time away from the manor while we are here."

Francine and Lisa exchanged questioning glances at one another. Lisa handed over the bowl apprehensively, and Francine set aside the pile of dirty dishes she was gathering. Lisa pointed to an ice cream stand across the way and rubbed her hands together in anticipation.

Addie could read the concern in Nora's furrowed brow, and the unease that oozed from her as her eyes darted around the park, taking inventory of each person's location. "Hey, I can only imagine how difficult this must be for you right now."

"True, it is beyond stressful, to say the least. Although, it doesn't compare to the unbearable agony at the thought of you being miles away from the manor." Nora's glassy eyes lowered their gaze to the table.

"At least I was in the safest possible location. Locked up in a cage and surrounded by police officers." Addie had hoped the intended joke would lighten Nora's spirits, but she immediately decided that comfort presided over humor in this situation. "I am eternally grateful that you confronted a debilitating fear to come bail me out."

Nora cringed. "To be completely honest, there was another reason."

"I know. It was really about Gregory having to fill out a statement at the station."

"Without the whole story, it was difficult to know who or what to believe."

"I completely understand." Addie reached across the table and squeezed Nora's hand. "Even before we spoke, you had provided a lawyer for me, and according to her, you had planned on not taking legal action against me."

"At that point, I really only had Gregory's side of what happened. By the time I had come across you yesterday, you were at the manor as well as the money, gun, and vehicle. I figured that I would offer you a lawyer and let the courts decide who was telling the truth between you and Gregory."

"That sounds logical, but what changed between then and Gregory's complete amendment to his written statement?" Addie looked over at him, looking very out of place in a park with a three-piece suit.

"Last night, I was too distraught over what had happened. I wanted no part in talking to anyone, so I spent the night hidden away in your bedroom. It wasn't until the ride here in the morning when Ruth presented me with your scrapbook, which helped unravel some of the missing links. Enough to know that I couldn't condemn you to jail time just because I was emotionally hurt."

"Somehow I doubt Gregory had a change of heart on his own accord."

"I think by now you've recognized that Gregory

had a little more than just an affinity for my father."

"He is quite protective of Mr. Rosin's personal items, I noticed."

"I highly doubt that my father reciprocated those feelings back, but he did regard Gregory as an esteemed assistant."

"I can see that he does a lot of the business aspect of work with you still."

"Yes, without him I wouldn't have been able to take over the company. I might have had to sell it off completely. He taught me everything I needed to know. I'm not sure if it is because he didn't want to see his beloved Mr. Rosin's business fail upon his death, or because he thinks he owes me for his life."

"His life?"

"Gregory was supposed to be on that airplane with our fathers. He accompanied my dad on almost all his business trips. It was a tiny plane, though, and since I had convinced my mother to join him, it left no room for him. He stayed behind, much to his dismay, that is, until he heard about the fatal accident."

"So was his statement clearing my name a trade off because Gregory believes he owes you for saving his life?"

"Believe it when I say that he has repeatedly reminded me that he has repaid me a thousand times over by obeying my wishes to stay on the manor grounds." Nora shook her head in annoyance. "What he fears is that if I were to ever no longer require his services, then he would also lose the manor itself."

"Just like you and I, it would be devastating to give up on all the memories of the person he loved."

"Exactly, so all I had to do was offer a little reminder to him that as a Rosin Manor employee, it was in his best interest to exercise our philosophy of maintaining a civil relationship with one another."

"That was beyond honorable of you not to take sides between someone you've trusted for years, and a new person who created a mess of things."

"I can't help but wonder that if Gregory had not been so accusing and suspicious of you from the very beginning, maybe you wouldn't have taken things to such an extreme level with him."

"I'd like to think things would have gone differently too." Addie rubbed at her neck in frustration with herself. "Look, I know that I broke the rules I was expected to follow, as well as your trust, but is there any possible way that you would be willing to give me a second chance? At both Rosin Manor and more importantly, with you?"

Nora closed her eyes and took a deep breath. She moved from the seat opposite from Addie and joined her on the same bench. "Can you promise me that you will talk to me and avoid any potential future events like we had in the last couple of days?" She stuck her pinky finger out to Addie.

Addie curled her finger around Nora's. "I promise." She pressed her lips against Nora's and confirmed the vow with a kiss. "I can't wait to go home with you."

"And I with you, although there's one thing you'll have to help me with first."

"Sure, what?"

Nora looked in almost every direction. "We need to somehow round up our very dysfunctional crew and convince them that it's time to go back home."

Addie joined Nora in a hearty laugh before coming together for another kiss.

Chapter Twenty-six

With all of them packed into the limousine together, Addie was amazed at just how spacious it still was. She had hoped to need to sit a lot closer to Nora, but there was so much room that it would have looked as though she was snuggling next to her on purpose. Finally able to have a happy reunion with Buddy, she figured that she could at least have him on her lap for the ride, but he seemed preoccupied with a burlap sack at Roger's feet. All attention seemed to be on the growling, little dog who kept pawing at the sack. There was a unanimous gasp from the crowd as something in the bag moved.

Henry, who was closest to the front of the car, tapped the driver on the shoulder through the open divider. "Don't pull away just yet."

Nora scooched forward on her seat to get a better view of Roger. "Please release whatever animal you have trapped in the bag back to the park."

Roger made an annoyed grunting sound, picked up the sack, and hulked over to the door. He gave the twine cord a tug so that it fell loose, keeping the opening shut with his fist. He flipped the sack upside down, let go of the top, and gave it a couple of vigorous shakes. Something fell out and its tiny claws made a scratching sound on the asphalt as it scrambled quickly away.

All heads of the passengers in the limo were

faced towards the tinted window on the side of the car where it escaped. A small gray squirrel scampered across the grass to the closest tree and shot up the trunk. It didn't stop until it reached the first limb, where it sat twitching nervously with watchful eyes, fearing capture again.

Lisa shook her head and let out a chuckle. "I guess you'll just have to settle for my cooking tonight, Roger."

The whole car erupted with laughter, except for Roger, who slunk back into his seat and sulked. Henry gave the signal to the driver that it was time to start their trip back to the manor. They had barely pulled away from the curb when Henry started to pass around the tall glass flutes and Lisa popped open a bottle of champagne. Ruth proposed a toast in honor of their first outing in over seven years, which elicited a round of cheers from all.

Everyone appeared to be in good spirits, except for Gregory, who was preoccupied with the contents of a large plastic bag. Addie watched as he rifled through it with a scrutinizing look. She wondered if she should offer an apology for what she put him through, or if she should thank him for what he did to help her get out of jail. There were too many ears listening in on them here, though, and she didn't want his response swayed by the audience. She hoped there would be plenty more opportunities in the future for them to talk and figure out how to co-exist amicably in the manor for Nora's sake.

After digging still, Gregory scrunched up his nose at something he came across. "I presume you'd like these back for your feet." He pulled out a pair of shoelaces dangling by two of his fingertips and tossed them in Addie's direction.

"Did you go back and get my personal items from the police station?"

"Mm, I wasn't sure if this little excursion out of the manor was a one-time event, so I made sure we tied up all loose ends in person while we were still here." Gregory couldn't be bothered to look up from his search of the bag.

"I'm surprised they handed over my things to you without my consent."

"Considering we just wrote them out a check to bail you out, they probably assume we are to be trusted to get a few vile items back to you." Gregory made a sour looking face as he pulled out the pizza delivery hat. He tossed it to the floor of the limo and wiped his hand off on the silk handkerchief in his suit pocket.

Roger's eyes lit up at the sight of the grubby hat. He plucked it from the floor, held it out in Addie's direction, and nodded.

"By all means, you can keep it." Addie shivered at the thought of how she couldn't wait to go home and wash her hair after having had the greasy object on her head for even a few minutes. She wondered if her bag had also been returned. "Hey, Gregory, is my bag in there too, by any chance?"

"As a matter of fact, it is, but it's still filled with Miss Rosin's money, so you can have it back when its contents have been emptied into the safe."

"Oh, so the story about the money being given to me to pay my college loans was just a fib to get me out of being locked up?" Addie gently nudged Nora's arm with her elbow and flashed a giant grin to show that her playful question was in jest.

Nora's face looked serious, though. She tilted her head and tapped a finger on her chin. "Gregory, did you complete that task I asked you about earlier?"

"The transaction went through as requested, Miss Rosin."

Nora turned her attention to Addie. "After your father passed, much of his financial profits were tied up in my father's business, since they were partners. I had to hire advisors and lawyers to split the earnings accordingly because your stepmother had to be bought out with her inherited shares."

Addie scowled at the thought of her stepmother. "That wretched woman knew how much building the business from the ground up meant to him. If she really loved him, she wouldn't have sold it off. I guess either way, it wouldn't have benefitted me, since he left me with nothing."

"Actually, that's not entirely true." Gregory's eyes were wild with excitement over the seemingly secret knowledge he possessed.

Typically, it would irk Addie when someone tossed in little snippets of cryptic information to a conversation without fully elaborating just for the sake of leaving you hanging. If she were not already treading on thin ice with an assault charge on Gregory, she would have gladly gone over and shook the words out of him. Instead, she looked between him and Nora for answers.

"I was still quite young during the start of the business negotiations and overwhelmed by trying to learn the process of running an entire operation just out of high school." Nora puffed out her cheeks and blew out an exasperated breath. "I had to sign off on stacks of paperwork that acknowledged that all funds from the business owed to Mrs. Krane were paid to her. There was, however, one small portion which had a stipulation attached to it, but I think I'll allow Gregory to explain it."

Addie turned to him, gripping onto the edge of the leather seat in anticipation of the story.

"As Mr. Rosin's trusted assistant, I spent a considerable amount of time traveling with both he and Mr. Krane. Your father spoke highly of you, but was disappointed in your lackluster enthusiasm for taking over his business someday."

"Ugh, what twenty-year old does?"

"He did, however, mention how proud he was that you were attending an Ivy League school with aspirations to become a doctor. He respected your career goals, which is why he prearranged for a specific will contribution for you. We were told to set aside the full tuition amount for your college education."

"Wait." Addie looked between the two of them, confused. "I met with the lawyer. He told me that I wasn't receiving anything. It all went to my stepmother, which is why I dropped out of college in the first place."

Gregory lifted his finger up so that she would give him the time to finish. "We were told to set aside the full tuition amount for your college education, with the contingency that it would be paid in full only on the day of your graduation. Furthermore, if you opted to continue another four years after undergraduate in a medical program, we were to wait until it was complete to pay that off as well."

Addie balled her hands up into tight fists. "If I had known any of this, I would have never left school in the first place."

Nora placed a calming hand on Addie's thigh. "We kept in contact with the college, waiting to see if you would complete your last year, or if you would transfer your credits elsewhere. They lost connection with you and you had already dropped off the grid, unable to be found."

"All I knew was that I had close to one-hundred-thousand dollars in debt to Harvard University and no one willing to support co-signing my loans. I realize now that I should have stayed and worked with financial aid to figure something out, but at the time, I was a scared kid without parents to hold my hand through the process, so I ran."

"With the money in limbo in an account we set aside, I started investing it over the years. On our way here, when we realized your identity, I had Gregory contact the school. We have officially paid off your debts despite the stipulation put in place by Mr. Krane. The invested money is enough to cover a little nest egg to either finish your education or start a new life."

The fact that she was officially free of any debt was liberating, to say the least, but it was the knowledge that her father hadn't actually left her behind without a care that brought a welling of tears to her eyes. "Thanks to you, a huge weight has been lifted off my shoulders. The world of opportunity is open to me once again."

Nora squeezed her hand. "I understand if you want to leave Rosin Manor. Your passion for wanting to be a doctor is a pursuit that cannot be attained out here."

Addie sat back in her seat. The trees they passed by were a blur of green. Yesterday, she had the same view, but as a criminal from the back of a police cruiser. Today, it was as a passenger in a limo with a group of people, none of which were related, but together formed a family. "I've lived my whole life in the city. I went from a skyscraper penthouse, to a bustling college campus, to the dank underground street life. I think I need a break to take things slow and learn how to breathe again. Sure, being a surgeon has its appeal, but there are other types of doctors, such as in the psychiatry field, where I can get my degree online while here at Rosin Manor."

Nora made a signal with her hand and the car slowed to a stop. She stood in a stooped position so as not to hit her head on the roof and extended her hand to Addie. "Care to join me for a stroll?"

Addie intertwined her fingers with Nora's and followed her out the door that the driver had opened. She nodded her head in thanks and they stepped aside so there was room for the car to pull back onto the road. She glanced at their surroundings to see the familiar gate along the road and when she followed it with her eyes, it wasn't too much farther to the driveway entrance. She could already hear the clanking as it slid open. Next to her, Addie could feel Nora's arm wrap around her waist and lead her to start their walk.

"How are you doing out here, or more importantly, how are you handling having me out here?"

"After the day we've had, this is much more tolerable." Nora set her hand over her chest and patted it. "Still a bit unsettling, but I consider it progress in the right direction."

"Thank you for running to me, instead of away from me, this time."

"It's all because you recognized the root of my

fear and gave me the push I needed to take the scary leap out of it." Nora paused momentarily to glance up at Addie and flash her a wink. "I'd say the new career path you've chosen is perfect for you."

Addie could feel an intense mixture of emotions flowing through her. So as not to break down in tears or out in dance, she focused on one step at a time with the woman she cared so deeply for at her side, until they reached the gate. "It feels so good to be home again."

She took in a view of the grounds that had once appeared so perfect in every way to her. This time, Addie spotted tiny imperfections in the grass growing just over the asphalt or leaves that had fallen around the trees. She wondered if it was a result of the entire staff being disrupted from their regular chore schedule, or if she had just observed it the way she wanted to see it in her mind. A perfect place that she had dreamed of being a part of.

They stepped inside the gate, and Addie approached the keypad, but before she could press the close button on the gate, Nora covered her hand.

"I'd like to leave it open. That way people on the outside know they are welcome to visit Rosin Manor and people on the inside know that they are free to leave, including you and I."

Addie slid her hand away from the keypad and wrapped it around Nora's waist to pull her into an embrace and to leave a kiss on her lips before they walked the rest of the way home together.

IF YOU LIKED THIS BOOK...

Share a review with your friends or post a review on your favorite site like Amazon, Goodreads, Barnes and Noble, or anywhere you purchased the book. Or perhaps share a posting on your social media sites and help spread the word.

Join the Sapphire Newsletter and keep up with all your favorite authors.

Did we mention you get a free book for joining our team?

sign-up at - www.sapphirebooks.com

About the author

Sarah Turtle spent the beginning portion of her childhood living in a small Maine island community, much like the setting in her debut novel, Laurel Cove. She moved around to other locations far from the East Coast, such as San Diego, but eventually came back to live in her home state of Maine. She just couldn't imagine not being able to enjoy the rocky coastline of New England, or the cold winter blizzards that she loves more than anything.

When she's not busy writing, Sarah loves going on bike rides, playing board games, video games, painting, and playing a variety of musical instruments. Faithfully by her side in all things, is her Jack Russell Terrier dog, Guinn.

Facebook - SarahTurtleAuthor
Twitter - @writergrrl78

Check out Sarah's other book

Laurel Cove - ISBN - 978-1-948232-53-1

Willa Barton has established herself as a successful author and screenwriter, residing in New York City, a stark contrast from her childhood upbringing in the small island community of Laurel Cove, Maine. Twenty years have passed since Willa's best friend, Brynn, kissed her, which resulted in Willa accidentally causing permanent injury to Brynn. After being shamed out of town for destroying the future of Laurel Cove's star athlete, Willa kept her distance; that is, until she receives a call that her father has passed away.

Willa's plan is simple—she is only going back long enough to tie up loose ends for her father's estate, sell his house, and attend his funeral. What she doesn't account for are the past grudges that still exist, a love that was never completely lost, and prospects of friendship. Can Willa right past wrongs to fulfill a promise from the grave so her father can be laid to rest?

Other Sapphire books from Sapphire Authors

Keeping Secrets – ISBN – 978-1-952270-04-8

What would you do if, after finally finding the woman of your dreams, she suddenly leaves to fight in the Civil War?

It's 1863, and Elizabeth Hepscott has resigned herself to a life of monotonous boredom far from the battlefields as the wife of a Missouri rancher. Her fate changes when she travels with her brother to Kentucky to help him join the Union Army. On a whim, she poses as his little brother and is bullied into enlisting, as well. Reluctantly pulled into a new destiny, a lark decision quickly cascades into mortal danger.

While Elizabeth's life has made a drastic U-turn, Charlie Schweicher, heiress to a glass-making fortune, is still searching for the only thing money can't buy.

A chance encounter drastically changes everything for both of them. Will Charlie find the love she's longed for, or will the war take it all away?

Diva – ISBN – 978-1-952270-10-9

What if...you were offered a part-time job as the personal assistant to someone you have idolized for years? Meg Ellis has just completed the school year as a nurse in the Santa Fe school system. It isn't her first choice of profession, but a medical problem derailed her musical career years ago. The breakup of a bad relationship is still painful. The loving support from her close-knit family and good friends has buoyed her spirits, but longing still lurks below the surface. She can't forget the intoxicating allure of the beautiful diva who haunts her dreams.

Nicole Bernard is a rising star in the world of opera, adored by fans around the globe. When Meg learns that Nicole is headlining a new production at the renowned New Mexico outdoor pavilion—and then is asked to accept a job offer to be her personal assistant—she is beside herself. After a short time learning the routine and reining in her hormones, Meg discovers that Nicole's family will be visiting for the opening. Her responsibility to the charismatic singer immediately becomes more difficult when Nicole's young husband Mario shows up and threatens the comfortable rapport between Meg and the prima donna.

The two women brace for a roller-coaster interlude composed by fate. Will the warm days and cool nights, the breathtaking scenery, and the romance of the music create summer love? A heartbreaking game? Or something very special?